Knitting

New Beginnings Book 4

ROBIN MERRILL

New Creation Publishing

Mercer, Maine

Scripture quotation from World English Bible.

For you formed my inmost being.
You knit me together in my mother's womb.
—Psalm 139:13

Prologue

Jason

Jason had come to the church to pray, but now that he was there, there was no prayer—only panic.

He sat silently, staring at the large wooden cross hanging in the front of the sanctuary.

Finally, he breathed, "Oh God, you must be so mad at me."

Predictably, God didn't answer. That was probably a good thing because if God was angry, Jason didn't want to hear what he had to say. He closed his eyes. There was no *if* God was angry. God was definitely angry.

He bowed his head. "I don't know what to say," he whispered. Only a few months ago he'd promised to follow Jesus. And then he'd gone and made the biggest mistake of his life. What had he been thinking?

He certainly hadn't been thinking about God.

"I don't know what to ask for," he whispered around the lump in his throat. "I really messed up, and I'm so, so sorry." A quiet sob erupted out of him, and he wiped at his eyes, embarrassed to be crying like a little boy. "I don't know what to do. I don't know what I need you to do. Just help me, God. Help me. I need you."

Chapter 1

Zoe

Zoe bent over and put her hands on her knees. She gasped for air, her lungs burning. What had she been thinking? Why had she gotten herself into this mess, and how was she going to get out of it? She feared it was going to kill her.

"Stand up straight!" Coach Hodges shouted.

Slowly Zoe uncurled herself.

The coach threw both her arms into the air, her eyes boring into Zoe's, not unkindly. She let the whistle fall from her lips. She spoke to all of them, though Zoe knew she was really addressing her directly. "Keeping your arms up in the air will make the cramps go away."

Zoe didn't have cramps, but she put her arms up anyway. She heard a snicker in the gym's balcony, and her eyes flitted that way. The boys' team was lined up for practice, which was great news because that meant that hers was almost over. Hype caught her eye and made a silent clapping motion. She knew he was trying to be supportive, but she was still annoyed and looked away. She scanned the line of boys for Jason, but he wasn't there. This was curious. He was never late for practice.

"Down and back two more times," Coach said, and Zoe thought she might cry. She sucked in a lungful of air and took off, already behind the rest of her team. Zoe had never been in good shape, and compared to her new teammates, she was in *terrible* shape.

She hadn't even wanted to play basketball. Jason had harassed her to no end, but she'd stood firm. When the season started, Zoe thought she'd dodged a bullet.

But the team only had eight girls, and Jason had brought the coach to Zoe's lunch table.

Coach Hodges was a persuasive woman.

Zoe made it to the baseline and turned for her second sprint.

"Great job, Zoe!" Coach called out, managing to sound sincere.

Before she'd reached half-court, though, Zoe met her teammates returning in the other direction. She didn't know what was going to kill her faster: the lack of oxygen or the embarrassment. She tried to go a little faster, but she wasn't sure that her feet cooperated. Coach Hodges had told her, "I can make you a ballplayer." Zoe had believed her. How stupid. If this was what ballplayers had to do, she wasn't going to last long. This was her third practice, and things weren't getting any easier. Her calf muscles had been so tight that morning that she'd cried walking to the bathroom.

Callie, a girl in Zoe's class whom she'd never talked to until she started playing basketball, got her team to start clapping and shouting for Zoe.

Zoe appreciated Callie's effort, but she wanted to be invisible. She didn't want to be the slow kid everybody went out of their way to encourage. The charity case.

Zoe had barely finished her sprint before Coach told them to bring it in. The rest of the team trotted and Zoe trudged toward the huddle. They put their hands together. Coach praised them and quickly reviewed their upcoming schedule. Zoe didn't really hear her words, though, because she was trying not to retch. Finally, they all flung their hands up into the air and shouted, "Family!"

Zoe turned to head to the locker room, but Coach stopped her. "Zoe? Would you mind staying for a few extra minutes?"

Zoe did not want to stay, but she couldn't make herself say that. Callie stood beside the coach, smiling. "Okay," Zoe said because she didn't know what else to say. The boys filed down the stairs, and the gym filled with the loud obnoxious chaos of a dozen bouncing balls. Zoe looked at her coach expectantly.

"I've asked Callie to spend a few minutes with you working on post shots."

Zoe managed to suppress her groan. It wasn't bad enough to be the worst kid on the team. Now she was being kept after class for extra help from the smart kid.

Coach registered Zoe's lack of enthusiasm. She stepped closer and lowered her voice. "I really appreciate it, Zoe. You're going to score a lot of points for us. We need to get you ready."

Zoe's brain didn't believe this promise, but her heart was encouraged. She nodded, and Coach walked away. Callie waved her over to a side hoop on the other end of the court. Callie stopped underneath the basket and took a small step to the side. "Coach wants us to practice shooting from right here ... like a thousand times."

Zoe didn't know what to say. This looked like a peewee basketball drill.

Callie laughed. "Don't be insulted. We've all had to do it. But if you shoot from here a thousand times, you won't be nervous when you have to do it in a game." She bounced Zoe the ball, and surprisingly, Zoe caught it. Callie glanced at the boys behind them. "Don't worry about them. They're all dorks."

Zoe laughed, once again wondering where Jason was, and shot the ball. It made a loud *dong* as it bounced off the rim, and Callie gave chase.

Chapter 2

Zoe

Zoe couldn't understand how Callie wasn't annoyed with this task she'd been given. Callie joyfully bounced the ball to her, and Zoe tried again. Again she missed. Again, Callie chased the ball. Again, Callie smiled as she brought it back. "Here," she said, a little out of breath. "Bend your knees a little and hold the ball like this. Then jump when you shoot and aim for that top corner of the square." She made it sound so simple. She handed the ball to Zoe for another try. Zoe stepped into her spot. She bent her knees, and her thighs screamed in protest. She held the ball like she'd been shown, and she jumped and shot. The ball banged off the backboard and went flying. She heard boys laughing. Callie was off at a sprint.

When she got back, she said, "Good job. You're getting closer."

Zoe wanted to laugh, but she was too tired. No. She wasn't getting closer.

"You don't have to throw it that hard. Just kiss it off the glass."

"Yeah, Zoe," Hype said from behind them. "Just kiss it off the glass."

His friend snickered, and Zoe considered beating them up, but decided she was too tired.

"Like I said, dorks. Go ahead. Give it another shot. Try it with a softer touch."

Zoe didn't know how to do anything with a soft touch. She shot the ball. It hit the correct part of the backboard and went through the net. Despite herself, Zoe found this incredibly satisfying.

"Yeah! Yay!" Callie cheered as if Zoe had just scored the winning shot. "Now bend your knees and jump this time."

Zoe bent her knees, jumped, and tried to have a soft touch. The ball hit the backboard too hard and bounced astray.

Callie fetched it. "You are so close, Zoe."

Zoe gave her an incredulous look. "What, are you like the most optimistic person on the planet?"

Callie giggled. "No, I don't think so." She bounced her the ball.

Zoe shot again. And missed.

When Callie returned with the ball, Zoe asked if they could quit.

"Let's do a few more. Trust me, it does get easier."

Easy for her to say. Callie was incredibly graceful and athletic, and she'd been playing basketball since she was five. All these girls had. Zoe sighed and shot the ball.

"You forgot to jump, but let's not worry about that part right now. You seem to not like the jumping. Maybe you don't need to. Do what you just did again."

Zoe shot again. It went in. She suppressed a grin. She didn't want to let on that she was excited about making a few baskets when she was hardly a foot from the hoop.

They shot these baby shots for thirty minutes before Callie announced that it was enough.

"Thank you," Zoe said softly.

"No problem. You want a ride home?"

Zoe did want a ride home. It was too cold to walk, and she didn't want to make Gramma come get her. "That'd be great."

Callie changed in record time.

"What's your secret to getting out of a sticky sports bra that fast?" Zoe was new to sports bras and found them shockingly easy to get trapped in.

Callie laughed. "I just leave it on. I'll deal with it later."

Zoe realized that Callie hadn't actually changed but had just put multiple layers on over her clothes. This seemed like a good plan. So Zoe stopped changing and started putting on lots of clothes instead.

When they got into Callie's car, she asked Zoe to remind her where she lived—as if she'd ever known.

Zoe was a little embarrassed to say she lived at 1 Providence Ave. Though it was an apartment building like any other, a lot of people in town considered it to be an old folks' home because only old folks lived there. But Callie didn't bat an eye.

They rode the short distance in comfortable silence until Zoe saw Jason's car parked beside the church. That was odd. "Actually, would you mind letting me off here?"

Callie looked surprised. "At the church?"

"Yeah. I know it's weird, but I spend a lot of time there."

Callie pulled the car alongside the curb. "Not weird. To each their own. See you tomorrow."

Zoe climbed out. "If I don't die of sore muscles first." She scooted down to look at Callie before slamming the door. "Thanks again for your help. Not sure why you got the job babysitting me, but I appreciate it."

Callie laughed. "I like winning. I volunteered to help."

Zoe wasn't sure what to say to that, so she shut the door and headed for the church. Why was Jason at the church and not at basketball practice?

Chapter 3

Esther

Esther was alone in the chilly basement of her beloved New Beginnings Church putting together food boxes. The grocery store had given them stacks and stacks of empty boxes, and Esther was currently filling them with goodies for local families. In each box she had put a bag of apples, a bag of oranges, a bag of onions, and some canned peas. She'd given a third of the boxes some cottage cheese, but then she'd run out of cottage cheese. Now she had her head in the fridge looking for something equitable to put in the cheeseless boxes. She thought she heard a voice and stood up straight, closing the fridge door. She didn't hear anything else and chalked it up to her imagination. She was about to open the fridge again when she heard Zoe say, "I thought I was the only weird one who hung out in empty churches on weekdays."

What? Who was Zoe talking to? Esther didn't hear anyone respond. Was her granddaughter up there alone talking to herself? If so, that couldn't be good. She could have been praying, but if so, she wouldn't be calling God a weird one who hung out in empty churches, would she?

She heard Zoe speak again. "Hey, what's going on? What's wrong?"

Then a male voice whispered something that Esther couldn't make out.

Feeling only a little guilty, Esther crept toward the stairs and then stared up at the open doorway, willing sound to do a better job of floating through it.

"What's that mean?" Zoe asked.

Esther put her foot on the bottom step but didn't ascend, knowing the stairs would creak and give her away. It was bad enough she was eavesdropping. It would be much worse to get caught.

The male voice said, "I'm not sure what to say." And Esther recognized the voice. Jason was there too? How long had he been there? Had he come in with Zoe?

"You say whatever's going on. You tell me what the problem is."

Again, silence. Then Jason said, "I can't." There was something about his voice. He didn't quite sound like himself. Of course, this made sense if he was upset about something.

"Of course you can. I'm your friend. I'll help."

Don't push too hard, Zoe.

They were quiet for so long that Esther thought they might have left. Then she heard Zoe say, "Jason, what is it?"

After another hesitation, Jason said, "Zoe, you are my friend, and I don't want to be rude, but I really just need to be alone right now."

"Okay," Zoe said, "but if there's anything that I can do to help, you'll ask?"

"You can't, but yeah, I would."

There was nothing else, and Esther thought that meant that Zoe had left. She stood there, her foot still on the bottom stair, wondering what to do next. She didn't want to get caught down here, not if Jason thought he was safe alone in his church. But she'd been puttering around down there for over an hour, and he hadn't known. She backed away from the stairs slowly and turned to go back to the fridge. She would just go back to her business, and if he caught her down there, she would play innocent and act like she hadn't heard anything.

But she had heard something. Or at least part of something. What had she heard, exactly? Jason was upset about something. She'd heard the concern in Zoe's voice. And he wouldn't tell her anything. This didn't necessarily mean it was a big deal. He just might not want to share with Zoe. But what did Jason DeGrave have to be upset about? He led a fairly charmed life. Of course, his parents were going through a messy divorce, but he seemed to be weathering that storm well. Was it something to do with basketball? She'd heard that he didn't like his new coach. But would that level of drama bring him alone to an empty sanctuary? She didn't think so. She shook her head. She shouldn't be trying to figure these things out. She grabbed some sour cream from the fridge and went back to the boxes. Not quite as yummy as cottage cheese but versatile.

As she placed the tubs into the boxes, she silently prayed, *Father, you know what's going on with Jason, and I know you're already right there with him in it. I just lift him up to you and ask for you to do mighty things for him and through him. Shower him with your favor and whatever he's struggling with right now, comfort him and give him your peace and your confidence. In Jesus' name I pray. Amen.*

She finished distributing the sour cream, stopped, and looked at the stairs. Maybe she should go up and talk to him. Maybe she'd be less threatening, and he'd open up to her. She shook her head. No, that was foolish.

Yes, she wanted to know what was going on with Jason because she cared about him and wanted to help. But she also wanted to know what was going on because she was feeling nosy. She was on the brink of acting like an old busybody.

"Sorry, Father," she whispered. "I'll try to leave this up to you. If you want me to interfere, you let me know."

Chapter 4

Zoe

Jason pulled his car in front of Zoe's apartment building as if everything was normal. Alita was hogging the front seat with a perky ponytail that Zoe desperately wanted to yank.

Zoe studied the back of Jason's head but couldn't glean any information from it.

It was hard to focus, though, because Alita was being such a chatterbox. Whether the perfect little princess wasn't aware that her boyfriend was acting strangely, was well aware and didn't care, or was trying to make up for his silence with her jabber, Zoe didn't know. But Jason didn't say a single word all the way to school. Zoe had tried to show restraint the night before and had only texted him once before she'd fallen asleep. "Hope you're feeling better. Remember, I'm just a shout away."

Not surprisingly, he hadn't responded.

He pulled into the school parking lot, and Zoe unfolded her sore body from the back seat to follow the loving couple into the school. Why did she do this to herself? Riding to school with them every single day put her in a bad mood every single morning. She knew why she did it. She wasn't proud of it, but it seemed she'd do just about anything to be close to that boy.

She went to her locker but kept an eye on Jason. He moved slowly, and his face was expressionless. He did not interact with Alita at all. She didn't seem to mind.

Zoe and Jason had every class together, so Zoe was able to continue analyzing his behavior throughout the day. He did ask her if she had an extra pencil during math, which she found encouraging. But then the day was over, and it was time for another hour and a half of torture in the name of the bouncy orange ball, and she was no wiser about Jason's problem.

She got into her practice clothes, put her earbuds in, and went into the gym to wait for the festivities to start. Her long legs dangled off the edge of the stage, swinging to the beat of the music. Her chattering teammates gathered around her, and she turned the music up.

Her playlist ended, and she picked up her phone to start another one.

Chevon sat beside her, whispering to the girl on the other side of her. Zoe wasn't paying any attention, but then she heard Jason's name and her entire body focused on what was coming out of Chevon's mouth. "No one knows, and you can't tell anyone," she whispered. "He would kill me."

The other girl responded, but Zoe couldn't make out what she said. She fought the urge to slide closer. Why did Chevon know what was going on with Jason and she didn't? This made her stomach hurt. Maybe she and Jason weren't as good a friends as she'd thought.

"Does he have a plan?" the friend asked.

"Yeah, it's called come up with a thousand bucks."

Coach Hodges blew the whistle, and the girls trotted toward her. Slowly, Zoe joined them. What had she just heard? A ball of lead settled in her stomach as her mind birthed a theory.

She didn't like this theory.

She told herself she shouldn't make assumptions. Just because Jason was a teenager didn't mean he was going to live out a script of some cheesy movie. She tried to talk herself out of her theory. Maybe he'd lost a bet. Maybe he'd borrowed money from someone and had to pay them back or he was going to get hurt. Maybe he got in trouble with the law and had to pay a fine. Any of these would be better than what she was thinking. But she didn't think any of these theories held water. First, why would he keep stuff like that from her? And none of those things sounded like Jason.

Of course, neither did impregnating Alita.

She tipped her head back to keep tears from falling. Of course they'd been sleeping together. How had she thought anything else was the case? Because she'd convinced herself that Jason was a good little Jesus boy who wouldn't be having sex.

She'd been wrong.

"Line up for the three-man weave!" Coach Hodges called.

Zoe actually knew what this was, but she didn't have the mental space to be proud of herself. She was too busy trying to figure out another meaning for those words she now wished she hadn't overheard.

But she could only come up with one. Alita was pregnant. And this was the worst news Zoe had ever heard in her entire life.

The ball hit her on the chin. This was entirely her fault, but the coach hollered at the girl who'd thrown it, telling her to say Zoe's name before she threw it. "In fact, everyone say the name of the person you're throwing it to! Let's go!"

Zoe felt the girls' annoyance at this new addition to the drill and wished Coach wouldn't work so hard to protect her. She got the ball back and threw it to the girl at midcourt, desperately wanting to get out of this gym, out of this school.

Her throat was nearly swollen shut. As if trying to run and breathe wasn't hard enough without the crying. She'd known she never had a shot with Jason. It's not like they were going to get married one day and have babies of their own, but this certainly made that reality more real. Alita was pregnant. She'd finally managed to trap Jason for the rest of his life. And the worst part was that Alita was happy about it. More than happy—giddy even. She'd been *giddy* on the way to school. Zoe should've pulled that stupid perky ponytail after all.

Chapter 5

Zoe

This time when Coach Hodges asked her to stay after and shoot peewee baskets with Callie, Zoe said, "No, thank you." In the last hour and a half, she'd decided to quit basketball altogether. She'd only been playing because Jason had wanted her to. She was glad now for a reason to quit. She hated it. It was stupid. It was a stupid game that made her stupid body hurt in stupid places.

When Callie, with a frustratingly concerned look on her face, offered Zoe a ride home, she said no thanks again.

She was going to walk. It was only twenty-four degrees out, but she was going to walk.

In a brokenhearted huff, she walked all the way to Main Street and into her favorite gas station. She ducked into the bathroom, shook her backpack open, ran the sink in case anybody was listening, and then left the bathroom sixty seconds after she went in.

Keeping her eyes on the register and not on the liquor bottles, she slyly reached out with one hand and wrapped her fingers around the neck of a fifth of vodka. Her mouth watered at the feel of it. She couldn't wait to feel that fire slide down her throat, but as she pulled it toward her, warm fingers wrapped around her wrist. She stopped and jerked her head toward whoever had just interfered with her little plan and found herself looking into the eyes of Levi.

"Oh, hi," she said, a little embarrassed. She let go of the bottle.

"You know, I can't recommend that brand," he said with a lazy smile.

She rolled her eyes. "I wasn't paying attention to the brand," she muttered.

He stepped closer to her. "I know that." He looked past her toward the door. "You want to go for a ride?"

She scowled. "You don't have a car." Instantly she felt guilty. Maybe he'd gotten one. Maybe he'd borrowed one. "Sorry."

He shrugged. "No need to be sorry. I'm not offended. I'm proud to be driving my mom's car around." He flashed that same smile. "So? A ride?"

"Wait. Can you even drive?" She looked down at his cast.

"Sure. I don't use both feet to drive. Do you?"

"I don't drive," she said softly.

"What?" he barked. He started toward the door. "Come on, if I'm faster than you, something is wrong."

Something was wrong. Her legs weren't broken, but they might as well have been as much as they hurt. Because she didn't know what else to do, she caught up. Maybe he had booze in his mom's car.

He pushed the big glass door open for her. "Why don't you drive?"

"Never took driver's ed."

He nodded and headed toward a nearby car. "Well, you need to hurry up and do that. Carver Harbor is boring enough *with* wheels, let alone without."

She got into his car, suddenly aware of how sweaty she was. "Maybe I should just go home."

"I can take you there, or we can go for a ride."

"A ride to where?"

"Anywhere you want." His eyes fell on his console. "Anywhere that an eighth of a tank of gas will take us." He laughed at his own joke.

Despite her shattered heart, she smiled.

"So, were you going to pay for that booze or just walk out with it?"

He had to know the answer to this. She didn't look twenty-one. "Don't have any money."

"I had a feeling." He started the car. "You a big drinker?"

She leaned back in the seat. "Used to be. Trying to turn over a new leaf."

He laughed heartily. "Oh yeah? How's that going?"

She laughed. "It's not as easy as it sounds."

His voice grew serious. "Tell me about it. I'm still on some drugs for the ankle and some other stuff, and they keep ordering me over and over again not to mix it with alcohol. I don't even know if it's that dangerous, but that warning gives me a little extra motivation." He took a deep breath as he pulled out onto the street. "I'm hoping I can continue with this sober streak once there is no more medication involved."

"That's good," Zoe said and then felt lame. "Good for you."

He looked at her and gave her that same smile. One side of his lip curled up more than the other, and his face was super relaxed. His laid-back nature calmed her heart rate a bit.

"So, you okay?"

"I'm fine."

"Cool." It was clear he didn't believe her. "I'd offer to go to the Cove but I'm afraid there might be people there drinking, since, you know, it's after dark in Carver Harbor."

She giggled. "Yeah, if you're trying to stay sober, that's not a safe place."

"Not a safe place for your new leaf. Hey! I heard about this really cool haunted cabin with no floor up in the woods. You want to go check that out?"

She laughed for real this time, and it felt great. Her heart was still shattered, but it was hurting a little less. "No, thank you. Already got that T-shirt."

He laughed as if that were the funniest thing he'd ever heard.

She found this exceptionally rewarding and tried to calm her own smile down a bit.

"Well, I'd offer to take you to the Ice Cream Scoop, but that closed months ago. You want a doughnut?"

"No, thanks. I eat enough doughnuts at church."

"Oh yeah? Doughnuts a big part of the Jesus gig?"

"Sort of." She looked at him. "You're welcome to come, you know. Anytime." She'd seen his mom in church, but she'd yet to see Levi. Suddenly she felt self-conscious. "I know, I know, girl steals a bottle of vodka and then invites you to church. What a hypocrite."

He laughed. "No, I was thinking no such thing. I was thinking that yeah, I should go to church soon. I've been meaning to. But it's so easy to stay in my pajamas and watch television. Hey! Let's take a ride out to Richie's Head. See if the lighthouse is still there."

She didn't know if he was joking and didn't dare to laugh, but then that smile appeared again. "Sure. We should go check because if it's not there, we should definitely tell someone."

"Oh, absolutely. We've just got ourselves a pressing mission." He stepped on the gas.

After a few seconds of uncomfortable silence, Zoe asked, "Have you heard any weird rumors about Jason lately?"

The smile slid off Levi's face. "Nope, sure haven't." He waited a beat and then asked, "Why?"

"No reason." She knew he wasn't buying that, so she added, "I just thought I might've heard something and was wondering if I misheard." Her cheeks got hot, and she twisted her fingers together nervously. "Never mind. I'm being dramatic, and I hate that."

"Not dramatic. Just in love."

"What? No," she said too quickly.

"It's okay. The whole town's in love with Jason DeGrave."

"Well, I'm not." She tried hard to mean that.

"You can lie if you want, but I've seen the way you look at him."

Now she was mad. Of course she was lying, but still, he didn't have the right to tell her how she felt as if he knew more about her feelings than she did. "Not much point to being in love with him when he's in love with Alita."

Levi didn't say anything for a while, but then he said thoughtfully, "I don't think Jason is in love with Alita." Zoe's heart leapt at this. She opened her mouth to say something, but Levi didn't let her. "But even if he wasn't dating her, I still don't think you should be in love with him."

She looked at him sharply. Did he know something about Jason that she didn't know? "Why's that?"

Levi gave her an unnerving gaze, the dashboard lights making the green in his eyes shine. "You know who Jason's in love with?"

Alita? Zoe shook her head.

"Jason DeGrave is in love with Jason DeGrave. Always has been, always will be." He turned his attention back to the road in front of him.

Zoe wasn't sure what he meant and didn't know how to respond. "Do you mean to say that he's cocky?"

Levi thought for a few seconds. "Nah, I wouldn't say that. He might be, but that's not what I meant. I just meant that with Jason, he's always going to be his own number one." He looked at her again. "And I would think that you would want that for yourself."

"Want what?"

"Don't you want to be someone's number one, Zoe?"

Chapter 6

Zoe

Z oe yawned.

"You sleep okay last night?" Gramma asked.

"Yeah. It's just early." Part of this was a lie. She hadn't slept well. She hadn't been able to stop thinking about Levi, which was a new problem. Usually when she couldn't sleep, it was Jason commandeering her thoughts. But Levi had been so unexpectedly weird the night before. He'd been so nice, and what had he meant with that stuff about being someone's number one? Surely he didn't like her? No one liked her. Granted, Levi wasn't the best-looking guy on the block, so maybe he'd have lower standards than a guy like Jason, but still. Levi could get lots of girls. He wasn't going to want Zoe. And even if he did, what did it matter? She didn't like him in that way.

"A penny for your thoughts?"

"Just wondering why Jason couldn't drive me this morning. Thanks again, by the way."

"Of course, honey. I'm never going to balk at the request to drive you to Bible study."

She didn't even know if she wanted to go to Bible study if Jason wasn't going to be there.

"Is Vicky nice to you guys while you're there?"

"She's never around. I mean, I think she's there because it's her house, but we don't see her. It's a big house. I think she has places to hide."

Esther chuckled. "Good. I love Vicky, but I'm not sure how much you should be exposed to her."

This was a welcome distraction from her thoughts about Levi. "What *is* wrong with her? I mean, I know she loves Jesus and everything, but she's so *mean*."

"She can be mean. She's very short, and I don't think she thinks before she speaks." Gramma chewed on her lower lip. "To some extent she's always been like that, but I think she is getting a little more crotchety with her old age ... Yeah, I don't know the answer to your question. I do know she loves Jesus and I know she does a lot of good things for a lot of people. For example, letting Emma and Tonya live with her. That's a huge thing. But you're right, if we didn't know better, we might think Vicky was mean enough to bite."

Zoe pictured Vicky on all fours chasing after someone trying to bite them and giggled.

They were quiet the rest of the way to Vicky's house. As Gramma pulled into the driveway, she said, "I'm really proud of you, honey. I know it's hard to get up early to study the Word, but it's really good that you're doing it."

Zoe felt a little guilty. She didn't go to Bible study on Thursday mornings because she hungered for the Word so much as she wanted to spend that extra time with Jason—without Alita. And she liked to hang out with Emma, whom she would only see on Sundays otherwise.

"Thanks, Gramma. Love you." Zoe got out and went to the door. Everybody greeted her, and she sat at the kitchen table.

Someone offered her a chocolate glazed doughnut, and only then did she think that she should've invited Levi. Of course they had invited him to Bible study before, but she'd had the perfect opportunity the night before and she hadn't even thought of it. She closed her eyes. She was a horrible Christian.

Hype read their scripture, tripping over a third of the words, and then Emma said a couple intelligent things about it, but Zoe had a hard time focusing. She couldn't stand not knowing. What if Alita wasn't even pregnant and she was doing all this grieving for nothing? She had to know for sure.

Hype drove her from Bible study to the high school. As she was trying to think of a way to ask him about Jason, he said, "Do you have any idea what's wrong with Jason lately?"

Stunned, she shook her head. "I don't. Was hoping you did."

"Do you really not know or are you just not telling me because it's a big secret?"

Zoe liked the idea that Hype thought Jason would trust her with his secrets. But he was so wrong. Apparently he trusted Chevon more than he trusted Hype or her. And why? *Wait.* Maybe Jason hadn't told Chevon. Maybe *Alita* had. Yes, that had to be it. "No, I really don't know anything."

"But would you say that anyway, even if you did know?"

She sighed. "I have no idea. I'm too tired to think about how I would act if I knew what I don't know."

He nodded solemnly. "Fair enough. But if he hasn't told me, and he hasn't told you, then probably he hasn't told anyone."

Again she was proud that Hype was including her in Jason's inner circle. "I don't know what it is, and I'm pretty worried about it. If you find out, will you tell me?"

Hype nodded. "Probably."

This wasn't good enough. "Hype, I'm serious."

"I know. So am I."

They got to the high school, and Zoe found Jason at his locker alone. Relieved that Alita was nowhere in sight, she walked up to him and punched him in the shoulder. "Hey, stranger. Why'd you skip Bible study?"

He looked at her, and his eyes were puffy and red. Had he been crying? "I told you. I don't feel good."

Zoe opened her mouth to say something, but no words came out.

Jason gave her a sad look and then turned and walked away. She watched him go, expecting him to head toward their first class early, but instead, he walked right out through the front doors.

Zoe hurriedly shoved everything into her locker and chased after him.

Chapter 7

Jason

Jason threw his car in reverse and backed out of his parking spot in a mad haze. He slammed on the brakes, put it in drive, and started to peel out when he saw Zoe running toward his car. He shook his head. That girl. Maybe he should just tell her. He needed to tell *someone*, or he was going to explode. He put his foot on the brake and waved at her to get in. She was probably the safest person *to* tell. Though he didn't want to think about how upset the news was going to make her. He knew how she felt about him.

She hadn't even shut the door behind her before the questions started. "What on earth? What is going on? Why won't you tell me anything?"

"Stop! You're making my head hurt."

She flinched and jerked back.

His heart sank with guilt. "I'm sorry. I'm not mad at you. I just haven't slept in a really long time, and ..." He didn't know how to finish his explanation.

"Life is so overwhelming that you're not sure if you're going to survive the next two minutes?"

He looked at her, surprised. "Yeah, pretty much. What makes you so insightful?"

She shrugged. "I've dealt with my fair share of overwhelmed moments. But Jason, this isn't like you."

Slowly, he started driving. Only because he couldn't be sitting in the middle of the parking lot when the first bell rang. "Maybe you don't know me as well as you think you do."

Again she looked hurt.

Maybe he should just stop talking so he could avoid hurting her. "I'm leaving. You want to go back in, so you don't get into trouble?"

She pulled the seat belt down and snapped it into place. "Where are we going?"

He shrugged and started driving.

"I'm going to try to make this easy on you," she said.

Despite his fondness for the girl, he was irritated.

"I think I know what's wrong, so I'm just going to guess."

"Okay," he said, pretty confident her guess would be about a mile wide of goal.

"Does it start with P and rhyme with regnant?"

His head jerked toward her. "Who told you?"

"No one," she said quickly.

He didn't believe her. No way she would just guess that. "Who told you, Zoe? I need to know because I need to know who knows because we have to keep this quiet."

She held her hands up. "I swear, Jason. No one knows. I was just trying to guess what would have you so upset and so secretive. And I might have overheard Chevon talking about it."

"What?" he cried. "Talking about it to who?"

Zoe hesitated. "I don't remember." She sounded angry, but he didn't have the energy to care why.

Jason groaned. "We have no idea how many people know then."

"I don't think many people know. I haven't heard anyone else talking about it."

He pulled over to the side of the road, put the car in park, and reclined his seat a foot. He threw his arm over his eyes. "Please don't tell anyone."

"I won't."

He turned his head so he could peek out at her from under his arm. "I'm serious. You can't tell anyone. Even Esther." He closed his eyes and muttered, "Especially Esther." He was going to die of shame if and when the church ladies found out.

"I won't tell anyone, I promise." She lowered her voice. "What are you going to do?"

What a dumb question. If he had any idea, he wouldn't be so terrified. "I don't know," he said without opening his mouth.

"Do your parents know?"

Another dumb question. "No, and I can't tell them. They are so caught up in their own garbage. This might kill them. Especially my dad. My poor father had to move to Bucksport, and he wouldn't let me go with him because he didn't want me to mess up my future." Jason grunted. "My *future*. What future? I don't have a future anymore."

"That's not true."

"Zoe, yes, it is. I could've played Division I, and now what? Now, not only will I not get a college scholarship, I won't even be able to go to college."

"I'm surprised she's decided to keep it," Zoe said slowly.

Jason groaned. "She hasn't. That's one of the things that's freaking me out. She doesn't want to keep it." His voice cracked.

"Part of me wishes she *would* just take care of it. Even though the guilt would probably kill me, at least it would be over, and I wouldn't be trying to figure out what to do. I wouldn't be trying to solve this unsolvable problem."

Zoe didn't say anything, and he realized he was desperate for her to say something, anything.

"Is Emma's father still living at your house?"

Okay, maybe not *anything*. "No. My mom got smart and kicked him out. It's the only thing I've got going for me right now. I think she was afraid I was going to beat him up again." This wasn't true, but he was trying to make her laugh.

It didn't work. "Do her parents know?"

"No. That's the only reason she hasn't done it yet. It's going to cost a thousand dollars, which she thinks I can just magically come up with somehow. Her parents' insurance would cover it, she thinks, but then they'd find out so she can't use their insurance. So she needs cash. But like I have a thousand dollars just kicking around. What does she think I am, a drug dealer? I don't even know anyone who has a thousand dollars. It might as well be a million." He squeezed his temples together. "At least, that's what she's telling me it costs. I don't know if any of this is true. I don't know anything at all."

Chapter 8

Esther

Saturday morning found Zoe in one dark mood. In an effort to snap her out of it, Esther asked, "Do you want to do something fun today?"

Zoe grunted.

"Was that an answer?"

"Sorry. I think I just want to veg out today."

Esther accepted that for the first few hours but then she got annoyed with Zoe's grumpy "vegging out." Her idea of vegging out was sitting on Esther's couch eating junk food and staring at her phone. What a waste of a weekend. "What are your friends doing this weekend?"

Zoe grunted again. "I don't have any friends."

Aha. She was onto something. Of course Zoe had friends, so she must be mad at one of them. "Did you get in a fight with Jason?"

"I don't want to talk about it."

Something in her tone suggested that she *did* want to talk about it, so Esther tried to push. "You can talk to me, Zoe. I've been around the block a time or two. I might have some insight to offer."

"I'm sure you do, but I promised him I wouldn't tell."

Esther remembered what she'd overheard in the sanctuary. Jason really did have a big secret. And whatever it was, it had Zoe tied up in knots. She took a deep breath. "You know, secrets can be tricky."

Zoe didn't look up from her phone. "You're telling me," she muttered. Then she shoved another chocolate-covered potato chip into her mouth. Esther knew she shouldn't have bought those even as they went into the cart. She hadn't been wrong.

"People can get hurt," she added.

"I'm not going to get hurt. This is Jason's secret, not mine."

Esther sat down beside her. "Zoe, if he needs help and he won't tell anyone, no one can help him."

She shook her head. "He doesn't need help."

Esther tried to figure out the riddle, but she wasn't a very good detective. "Should I call his mom? At least offer to help?"

Zoe's head snapped toward her. "No!" she said loudly. "Don't call anyone! I've already said too much. He's going to hate me if you interfere. He'll never tell me anything again."

So he was in trouble. Try as she may, though, she couldn't figure out what a boy like Jason could get in trouble doing. Then it hit her. He had girl trouble. "Is this about that little blond girlfriend of his?"

Zoe looked at her slowly. "Gramma, please. It's none of our business." She went back to her phone.

"If it's none of your business, then why are you spending your whole Saturday sulking about it?"

"I'm not sulking," she snapped. "I'm just worried about him."

Something about this didn't ring true. She might be worried, but that's not what had her upset. There was something else, but

Esther couldn't quite put her finger on it. "Remind me of the young lady's name?"

Zoe grimaced and said, "Alita" with malice.

"Zoe, I know she's not a very nice girl, but Jesus doesn't want us hating people."

"Jesus doesn't know what she's like."

Esther laughed and then felt bad for laughing. Maybe Zoe really didn't know better than that. "Child, of course he does. God made Alita just like he made the rest of us."

"Well, he made a mistake with that one."

"What's so bad about her?"

"She's stuck up, cocky, and mean. And she's not nice to Jason. She's going to ruin his life."

Esther patted her knee. "I wouldn't be so sure about that. Most people don't marry their high school sweethearts. Jason's going to grow up, leave Carver Harbor, and I'm willing to bet he will leave Alita behind." She held up her hands. "I'm not saying that I hope this is so. Maybe she'll go in her own direction and leave him behind. But one or the other is usually the way these things work."

Zoe gave her a cryptic look and said, "I'm not so sure."

"Not sure about what, that he'll leave Carver Harbor or that he'll outgrow Alita?"

Zoe looked positively devastated as she said, "Both."

What? "I thought Jason had big college plans."

"Not anymore," Zoe mumbled, and all the puzzle pieces clicked into place in Esther's mind. Or maybe the Holy Spirit revealed it to her. Either way, she knew what was going on.

There was a baby.

Esther stared at Zoe, wondering if she should confirm her theory, but she didn't want to stress the child further. So she got up and went into the kitchen to putter.

Six minutes later she went and stood in front of Zoe. "Is Alita pregnant?"

Zoe's head jerked up, her face confirming it even if her mouth wasn't about to. "You can't tell the others."

"I understand, but we can help."

"Gramma, seriously. He specifically said he didn't want you guys to know. He's pretty ashamed."

"Oh bosh. Men have been getting themselves into this kind of pickle for thousands of years." This was true, of course, but even as she spoke the words, she knew they would bring no comfort to Jason. He was probably a mess, drowning in shame and fear. "His parents don't know?"

She shook her head.

"Do hers?"

Zoe shook her head again.

"So no one knows but you?"

A tear escaped the corner of Zoe's eye, and Esther realized what really had this child all torn up. She was in love with the boy. She was in love with the boy who was going to marry someone else.

"Maybe you should tell them that we're here for them. You don't have to tell them that we know yet. Just comfort them with the fact that we will be behind them and will help. That should make him less scared—"

Zoe shook her head. "I'm not telling *her* anything. She wouldn't listen to me even if I tried. Besides, there's nothing to help with. This will all be over soon."

Esther's stomach rolled. Oh no. "What does that mean?"

Zoe gave her a sad look. "You know what that means."

Esther paced back and forth across her small living room, trying to figure out what she should do. Zoe had a point. It wasn't any of her business, and she didn't even know Alita. But this was too serious to do nothing. These kids were about to make the biggest mistake of their lives, a mistake that could never be undone.

She went into her bedroom and knelt beside her bed. "Father, I don't know what to do here. Am I supposed to do something? Help me, Father. Help us. Help those kids. Give them hope and faith and courage and block the devil's lies from reaching their ears." She lowered her forehead to rest on the bed. "Please, Father, tell me how to help." No answer came, and she grew fidgety. She rose to her feet and paced in her bedroom for a few minutes, but this made her more anxious. She had to do something for her own sanity, but there was nothing *to* do.

So she went back into the living room, picked up the basket that sat on the end table by the couch, and sat down to do what she did every time she heard there was a new baby.

She started knitting.

Chapter 9

Esther

Fiona played beautifully, and Rachel led the singing with gusto, but Esther had trouble focusing on the music.

Jason wasn't in church.

She'd been afraid that he'd skip out, and he had. The good news was that Levi had come. He'd even left his mother sitting alone in the back pew and come up to sit beside Zoe, who looked a little shell-shocked by his company. But even that delightful development didn't distract Esther from worrying about Jason.

Then, no matter how hard she tried, she couldn't concentrate on the pastor's choppy sermon about Daniel. Or maybe it wasn't choppy. Maybe she was just tuning in and out—with a little more out than in. Near the end of the sermon, Walter gave her a concerned look. "Are you feeling all right?"

She nodded quickly and opened her mouth to say something about worrying about Jason but then snapped it shut. She couldn't tell Walter why she was worried about Jason. She couldn't tell anyone.

Finally the service was over, and Esther scooted out far earlier than she usually did. She went straight to her kitchen and preheated the oven.

When Zoe saw the pie crust in the pan, her eyes lit up. "What kind are you making?"

"Blueberry," Esther said and then as soon as Zoe turned around, she hurriedly put a second pie crust into a second plate. The original wasn't meant for Zoe, but she hated to disappoint.

They had ham salad sandwiches for lunch, and Zoe didn't finish hers. Esther knew she was saving room for her pie but didn't scold her for it. Blueberry pie was probably healthier than ham salad anyway.

When they'd finished their sandwiches, Esther went back to her knitting, anxiously waiting for the pies to finish.

"What are you making?"

Esther had been working on a collection of winter scarves to give away, but it was obvious from what she had so far that this was no scarf.

"Booties."

Zoe snickered. "Booties?"

"Yes. Baby booties."

Zoe's face fell. "You know there's not going to be any baby, right?"

Don't overreact, Esther told herself. "I know no such thing. All I know is that these situations are difficult, and we need to be patient, trusting that God will work things out for the best."

Zoe rolled her eyes. "I don't think Alita is going to let God do anything."

Esther bit her tongue.

Finally the pies were done, and Zoe cut into hers far too soon. The blueberries were still steaming.

"There's Breyer's vanilla in the freezer if you want some." Esther busied herself boxing up the first pie.

"Yes! Ice cream for the win!" Zoe leapt up and went to the freezer. She noticed what Esther was doing and raised her eyebrows. "Who's that for?"

Esther didn't want to tell her. "Pie delivery. You know me."

Zoe laughed. "I sure do. Are you going far?"

Esther shook her head quickly and turned to leave before Zoe asked any more questions. "I'll be right back. Enjoy your pie!"

"Aren't you going to have any?" Zoe called after her, but Esther pretended not to hear.

Milton met her in the elevator. "Who's that for?"

People sure were nosy when it came to pie. "Just a friend."

"I want to be your friend!" He laughed heartily.

"You are my friend. For sure, Milton."

"Then why don't I get pie?"

She stepped off the elevator and turned to look at him. "Let's just say this is for a friend who wasn't able to come to church today. So if you start coming to church, and then you miss a Sunday, I'll make you pie."

Milton opened his mouth, but the doors closed before he could say anything. She was pretty sure he'd meant to get off on the ground floor, but in his shock and confusion, he'd forgotten to do so.

Esther hurried to her car and made the short drive to Jason's house. She wasn't even sure he'd be home. She thought he moved back and forth between his parents' houses, but she had no idea where his dad lived now.

Jason's mom answered the door. Eying the pie, she asked, "Can I help you?"

"Hi, I'm a friend of Jason's, and I was—"

"*You're* a friend of Jason's?" The woman laughed critically.

Esther forced herself to laugh along. "I can see how that might be surprising. I go to church with Jason." She pointed in the general direction of her church. "And I was concerned—"

"My boy skips a single Sunday, and you people come to harass him?" She folded her arms across her chest. "I've heard that place is a new cult. Now I'm starting to believe it."

Jason appeared over her shoulder. "Mom, stop it. This is Esther."

"Esther," the woman repeated doubtfully.

Esther let go of the pie to extend her right hand. "Yes, Esther. It's nice to meet you."

The woman eyed the offered hand warily but finally took it. She probably found it too rude not to. "Alexis."

Jason stepped around his mother. "For real, Mom. This is Zoe's grandmother. She's really okay."

Thrilled to be deemed "really okay," Esther held the pie out to Jason. "Not here to harass you at all. We just missed you this morning. I figured you might be feeling under the weather, so I thought some blueberry pie would help."

Jason grinned, but there was suspicion in his eyes. "Thank you." He turned to go back inside. This wasn't working as well as Esther had hoped it would. She'd wanted to start a conversation, but she'd ended up just giving away pie. As he closed the door in her face, he said, "Thanks again." And now she was standing in front of his door like a dunce.

No harm done, she told herself on the way back to the car. Maybe it didn't do any good, but at least now there was more pie in the world.

But when she got back to the apartment, her theory about no harm was challenged. Zoe met her at the door. "I told you not to tell him!" she shouted.

"Lower your voice!" Esther said, horrified at her volume. "Don't you holler at me!"

Zoe lowered her voice. "Sorry, but Gramma! Jason is really mad at me. He hates me. What did you do?"

Esther took off her coat, hung it on the hook, and walked by her before answering. "I didn't do anything. I made the boy pie."

"Why would you make him pie?" Zoe cried as if that was the most offensive thing in the world.

Esther sat on the couch and picked up her knitting needles. "I figured he might like pie."

Zoe rolled her eyes so hard Esther feared she'd hurt herself. "Did you say anything?"

"No. I introduced myself to his mother and I handed him a pie and told him we missed him. That was it." She leveled a gaze at her granddaughter. "I didn't do anything wrong, Zoe."

"Fine. I'm going for a walk."

"It's freezing outside."

"I'm just going to the common room. I want to call Jason. He texted me, but I want to talk to him. Tell him you don't know or something."

"First, don't lie to him. Second, you can't talk to him here?"

"Of course not. I don't trust you right now." She stomped toward the door and then slammed it behind her.

Esther felt guilty but told herself that she shouldn't. She hadn't spilled any secrets. She hadn't stuck her nose where it didn't belong or interfered. She hadn't done anything wrong.

She let her needles rest in her lap, tipped her head back, and looked at the ceiling. She needed help with this. Who could she ask for advice? She loved her friends, but she didn't trust them not to gossip. Maybe she should tell Pastor Adam. He was young. He had training. He would know what to do. But did she know him well enough to trust him with something like this? Maybe he wouldn't know what to do. Maybe he'd make things worse. Just because he'd been great in one crisis didn't mean he'd be up for this one.

Chapter 10

Zoe

Zoe wasn't sure Jason was going to pick her up on Monday morning. He'd been so mad at her that he wouldn't even answer his phone. But he did pick her up and even acted somewhat normal, asking her how her weekend was, though it was hard for him to get a word in edgewise with all of Alita's babbling. Apparently, she'd gotten a hysterical pedicure the day before, accidentally spraying lotion all over the technician's face when the poor woman had unintentionally tickled Alita's wicked little toes. It was *so* funny that Alita had to tell the story twice because Jason didn't laugh hard enough the first time.

What was wrong with her? Was she performing for Zoe? Was she putting on a show so that Zoe wouldn't know she was secretly freaking out inside? Zoe didn't think so. Zoe didn't think this girl was freaking out about anything. This girl was acting just as dumb as she always acted.

When Zoe heard the announcement that there would be a cheerleading meeting at lunchtime, she thought maybe God had intervened for her. She would finally get to talk to Jason alone. If he still sat with her, that was.

Zoe sat bouncing her leg up and down waiting to see where he would go when he got out of the line, and as usual, he made a beeline for her. Unfortunately, Hype started coming too. He usually didn't sit with them because he didn't like sitting with Alita, but her absence was attracting him. Zoe tried to be subtle as she shook her head slowly back and forth. Hype got the drift and pivoted in another direction just as Jason sat down.

"I'm sorry," Zoe said. "Really. I didn't tell her anything. She figured it out."

"How did she figure it out?"

"Just like I figured it out. There's only so many things that could have a guy like you this upset."

Jason glared at her. "You had to tell her something before she could figure it out."

"Yeah, sorry. I'm pretty upset about this, and she saw that. I told her I was worried about you, and boom, she guessed."

Jason looked doubtful.

Zoe took a deep breath. "I'm sorry. She hasn't told anyone. She said that she won't. Now, has anything changed?"

Jason put a tater tot in his mouth. "You mean have I come up with a thousand dollars?"

"No, that's not what I meant. I mean, she's acting awfully happy, so I thought maybe something was different."

Jason scowled. "What do you mean, she's acting happy? She's not acting happy."

Zoe stared at him. Was he so self-absorbed that he wasn't aware of how his girlfriend was acting? Because she certainly wasn't acting scared. "Jason, I don't want to argue with you, but this might be the most disturbing part of this whole thing. Why are you all torn up and freaking out and thinking about how your life is over, and she's just having a grand old time giggling? Why isn't she freaking out along with you? Why is she busy getting pedicures and being mean to the nail technician?"

Jason dropped his fork, and color drained from his face. "Zoe," he said slowly. "Alita doesn't know."

Zoe had never been so confused. "What?"

"Alita isn't pregnant. Chevon is."

Zoe almost choked on her food. She coughed, took a drink of water, and got some semblance of control over herself. And then she said again, "What?"

He leaned closer to her. "I'm sorry. I thought you knew it was Chevon. You said you overheard her talking about it."

Dizziness washed over her. She didn't know if it was from the choking or from this new revelation. Not only had Jason slept with Alita, he'd also slept with Chevon, maybe slept with the whole school. Everyone but her, anyway. "You slept with Chevon?" she whispered.

He shushed her. "Keep your voice down, please. And yes. Obviously." His cheeks were red, but his embarrassment gave her no satisfaction.

"Why?" Zoe asked before she could stop herself.

Jason gave her a curious look. "I don't really know how to explain it. It just sort of happened."

"But do you even like her?"

"I didn't think so," Jason said slowly, "but now ... I don't know how to explain it."

"What does that mean?"

"I don't know what it means," he snapped. "I don't know what any of this means. I don't know anything. There's too many things going on in my brain."

Zoe tried to organize the facts in her own brain. "So Chevon is the one who wants to get an abortion, and Alita doesn't even know she's pregnant."

Jason nodded. "And I'd really like her not to find out."

"Are you seriously worried about that right now?" Zoe said too loudly. "Who cares about that?"

Jason's jaw tightened. "I cheated on her. I'm not proud of it."

"Does that mean you don't cheat on her all the time?"

"Of course not. Who do you think I am?"

"I have no idea who you are."

Jason reared back. "Zoe, that's not fair."

"Sorry," she mumbled. "I didn't mean it as mean as it sounded."

He took a long breath. "You're like my only friend right now. I can't exactly talk to Hype about this. And my only other female friend other than you is Chevon."

That news came like a knife to her heart. "And all she's saying about it is, 'Give me a thousand bucks'?"

"No, it's not like that. She's freaking out too. But she doesn't want to have a baby. Neither one of us do. We don't see any other way out of this."

Zoe was still worried about Jason, but the longer she sat there, and the more he talked, the angrier she got. She didn't know if this anger made any sense, but it was there, and it was intense. "Maybe you should schedule a time to tell Alita the news and charge people for tickets to the fireworks. Then you'd have your thousand."

For a second Jason just stared at her. But then he picked up his tray and walked away.

Chapter 11

Esther

Esther sat on her couch trying not to agonize over Jason's predicament. "Knit one, purl one, knit one, purl one," she muttered, trying to stay focused.

Zoe came through the door like a whirlwind smelling of sweat and McDonald's. She dropped her bags and collapsed on the couch beside her.

"It's not Alita."

Esther's needles paused. "What do you mean it's not her? He got a different girl pregnant?"

Zoe leaned back and closed her eyes, obviously exhausted. "Yes, that's what it means. Apparently Jason DeGrave gets around."

Esther didn't like the sound of that. "Who is she?"

"You don't know her."

"You don't know that. I know lots of families in this town."

"Well, I'm not going to tell you who it is. I just wanted to tell you that it wasn't Alita, so you don't bake her a pie." The words were pretty sassy, but Zoe's tone was gentle, so Esther let it slide.

"How was your game?"

"Terrible. I only played for like ten seconds, and I had no idea what was going on."

"Well, I'm sorry to have missed it."

Zoe opened one eye and looked at her. "No, really. I meant it. I didn't want you there. I'm embarrassed."

"Well, I hope you don't think you can keep me away from your home games. And you have nothing to be embarrassed about. You've never played this game before, and you are doing the best you can. You're part of a team and you're getting lots of exercise. You should be proud." Esther was certainly proud of her. And she couldn't wait to go to one of her games.

Zoe groaned. "All the coach wants me to do is make little baby shots, and I can't even do that."

Esther didn't know much about basketball and didn't know what to say to that. "You don't have to play next year."

"I shouldn't have played this year! But Jason ..." she started but then trailed off. She yawned. "So, I had an idea."

"Yeah?" Esther asked while counting her stitches.

"I know you're not going to like it and I feel like if you haven't already mentioned it then it's probably a no-go but just in case you haven't thought of it yourself, I thought I should mention it."

Esther could not imagine where she was going with this. "Go on."

"You know how our church gives money to people in need?"

"Sure."

Zoe looked at her. "Jason needs a thousand dollars."

Before she could catch on, Esther said, "For what?" But then she realized what Zoe meant and gasped. "Zoe, you can't be serious."

Zoe rubbed her forehead. "I don't know if I'm serious. It was just a thought. I'm trying to figure out how to help."

"Helping them get an abortion is not helping!" Calm down, she told herself.

"I'm sorry, Gramma. I know that people your age think abortion is this big crime, but I learned a long time ago that it is just a few cells at this point. It's really not a big deal."

Esther's heart nearly lurched out of her chest. No big deal? What was this child thinking? *She doesn't know*, a soft voice whispered into Esther's heart. *She doesn't understand.*

Esther put her knitting down and turned her body to face Zoe. "I don't know much about science. But I know that every single human being is unique. And I know that God designs them one by one to be unique. Brothers and sisters can be so different. That means that every single person starts out different. So even if this person in this girl's womb is just a few cells, it's still a person God has specifically designed. If that baby's heart isn't already beating, then it will be soon. Think about that, Zoe. There is a teeny tiny beating heart, designed by God, with a whole life in front of her. An abortion would kill that person. It would stop her heart from beating." She paused. "Abortion is murder."

Zoe looked thoughtful.

"Does that make sense?"

"I guess. Honestly, I've never really thought much about it."

"You shouldn't have to. And I didn't mean to get all morbid on you. But it's a very, very big deal. It's a matter of life and death."

Chapter 12

Esther

Carver Harbor's high school gym was bigger than it needed to be, a leftover from glory days gone by. After the mill closed, enrollment slowly shrank to half of its old numbers. Esther wasn't sure if people all over Maine were having fewer kids or if they were having just as many kids and just not having them in Carver Harbor.

So even though there were quite a few attendees at the girls' first home game, they were spread out across the gym, comfortably spaced. That is, everybody except for Walter, who sat so close to Esther she feared her cheeks were pink. Part of her feared he was going to hold her hand and send those pink cheeks closer to maroon. Part of her hoped he would.

All of a sudden music blasted from giant speakers on the stage, and Esther jumped as a girl with a basketball burst through a paper hoop. She was followed by her eight teammates, with Zoe bringing up the rear. She was pale as a ghost. Esther's heart swelled with pride as Walter leapt to his feet, shot a fist into the air, and shouted what sounded like a war cry. Now Esther was embarrassed for a whole new reason. She reached up and grabbed the hem of his shirt to try to pull him back down, but he ignored her and kept shouting Zoe's name. Zoe glanced up at him, but Esther couldn't tell if she was disgusted, amused, or pleased. Maybe some combination of the three. Maybe something else altogether. It wasn't always easy to read Zoe.

Finally Walter sat down. "I just want her to know she is supported."

"She does."

Esther noticed the Puddy family—all seven of them—walking down the sideline on the other side of the court. When they found a spot big enough, they clambered into the bleachers. Each kid wore big clomping boots that made an impressive ruckus. Esther tried to catch Lauren's eye, but she was too busy wrangling her kids into a small huddle.

"Do you think they come to all the games?" Walter asked thoughtfully.

"I doubt it." Though it did make for cheap entertainment, Esther couldn't imagine them going to the trouble of packing all their kids up on a weeknight. Although, maybe homeschool families didn't worry so much about bedtimes on weeknights. "Maybe," Esther said.

"Or maybe they're here to support Zoe."

"I think that's more likely." This made Esther think of Jason, and she scanned the gym before she realized that he was playing at Mattanawcook tonight. "Just how far away is Mattanawcook?"

"It's in Lincoln, so I don't know, almost two hours."

Lincoln. That's why she didn't know. It was so confusing when schools weren't named after their towns.

"These girls had quite a bus ride," Walter said.

Esther looked at the other end of the gym, at the shiny maroon warmups the visiting team wore. The girls all looked strong and healthy. "They don't look any worse for wear."

Walter looked that way. "They sure don't. Any idea how this game is supposed to go?"

"Nope."

"Well," Walter lowered his voice, "I hope it's a blowout either way, so Zoe can get to play some."

It took Esther a second to realize what he meant, but then she elbowed him playfully. "Don't say that you hope that they beat us by a hundred points."

Walter shrugged. "I just want Zoe to have a chance to shine."

Now that he mentioned it, Esther wanted that too. She watched her granddaughter go through the warmup drills, a little surprised at how not gawky she was. She wasn't graceful by any means, but she didn't look as uncoordinated as Esther had expected.

After one more too-loud song that Esther didn't recognize and didn't care if she ever heard again, the buzzer sounded, and the girls all ran to the bench in front of Esther and Walter. Zoe glanced up at her, and Esther gave her a smile that she hoped imbued confidence.

Within seconds it was clear that Carver Harbor was outmatched. Mattanawcook scored hoop after hoop. Carver Harbor's point guard—Esther thought her name was Callie—was working very hard and doing things that seemed smart, but the rest of the team seemed fairly flat. Esther tried not to think about it, but she couldn't help eyeing each girl individually. Was number five pregnant? Was it number twenty-two? None of them looked pregnant, but, of course, they probably wouldn't yet. She shook her head and tried to concentrate on the game.

This became easier when the coach put Zoe in. *Father, give her confidence. Help her do this.*

The point guard came right up to her and said, "Just like we practiced. I'm giving you the ball."

Zoe nodded, but Esther could tell she was terrified.

Sure enough, on the next trip down the court, the guard gave the ball to Zoe. Without dribbling, Zoe turned toward the hoop and shot. It hit the backboard and bounced in.

Walter jumped to his feet and screamed. Esther fought the urge to do the same. As she tried to pull Walter back down, she noticed a young man on the other side of the gym mirroring Walter's actions. It was Levi! He stood all alone clapping and cheering at the top of his lungs. Wow. Her Zoe was garnering quite a fan club.

Chapter 13

Jason

"Where's Alita?" Zoe asked as soon as she got into the car.

"Going to get her," Jason said. "I picked you up first."

Zoe stopped buckling up and looked at him. "You could have told me that before I got in the front."

"You can have the front."

She looked shocked. "Seriously?"

"I don't care."

"But won't Alita care? She's going to freak out."

"I don't care." Jason was having trouble caring about anything right now, anything other than Chevon.

As Zoe finished buckling up, Jason pulled away from the curb. "I wanted to talk to you before ..."

"Okay. Go ahead."

"I think I need to talk to Esther."

Zoe gasped. "Why?"

"Because I need to talk to someone," he snapped, "and you're not much help."

She didn't say anything at first. "Well, that was rude."

"Sorry. I just feel like she might have some advice. Chevon is just waiting for me to come up with the money, like I actually can.

But each day that goes by, that baby gets bigger." He hit his steering wheel so hard he hurt the palm of his hand. "I don't know what to do."

"I can tell you what not to do. Don't ask Esther for money."

"What?" Jason cried. "I wouldn't do that!" He waited for her to say something, but she didn't. "Why would you think I would do that?"

She shrugged. "I don't know. I wasn't saying that you were going to do it. I was just saying not to. I already did."

Reflexively, he stepped on the brake. He looked at her. "What?" he cried again. "Why would you do that?"

"Don't stop in the middle of the street. You have enough problems." She waved toward the road in front of them. "Come on, let's go."

He stepped on the gas again. "Seriously, though, Zoe, what were you thinking? Do you know how embarrassing it is that you asked her for money for me?"

"Oh, calm down. I thought we were desperate. Our church gives money to people in need, and I thought that you were in need."

"Zoe," he said, trying to stay calm though he was shaking like a cold puppy. "I'm pretty sure that our church thinks abortion is murder, so I'm pretty sure that they're not going to pay for it."

"Yeah," Zoe said through clenched teeth, "that's pretty much what she told me." She looked at him curiously. "Is it, though?"

"Is what what?"

"Is it murder? I mean really. I know that the old ladies think it is, and I guess that Christians think it is, but how can it be? It's like a blob of cells."

Jason shook his head. "I honestly don't know. Believe me, I've thought about it a lot lately. You're right. It is a blob of cells. But it's also so much more than that. I mean, it's a part of Chevon, and it's a part of me. It's a little person. I think that, even though it's a blob of cells, it's still a little person. I mean, we *made* that."

Zoe looked horrified.

"What?" He pulled onto Richie's Head Road. They had to wrap up this conversation soon.

"You sound like you actually want to have a baby."

Jason shrugged. Maybe he did. The more time he spent with it, the less absurd the idea seemed.

"But what about your *future*?" She said the word with a heavy dose of disdain. "You're going to be a big star and do great things. What about all that?"

"I don't know. That all seems really far away right now. Like that's someone else's life. And I don't think I want to leave Chevon."

They were quiet for a minute and then he pulled into Alita's driveway.

Zoe dramatically flung the seatbelt off, and it made a loud *crack* as it hit the window on her door. As she climbed out to get into the back she said, "Interesting that you don't want to leave Chevon. I've never heard you worry about leaving Alita. And yet she's the one you're dating." She slammed the front door, got into the back, and slammed that door too. "By the way, I scored six points last night. Thanks for asking."

He turned and looked at her. "Hey, would you cut me some slack? I'm not myself right now. I'm losing my mind, like literally. I'm scared that my father is going to find out and literally murder me. I'm scared I'm going to make the wrong decision and ruin both our lives. I'm actually considering stealing the money, which will make me a criminal. I think I should talk to Pastor, but I can't make myself. So I want to talk to Esther. Maybe she'll take me to see the pastor. I don't know ..." He turned toward the front. "I'm so tired of saying the words *I don't know*."

"What about your mom?"

"I hate my mother. I'm not talking to her about anything ever."

"Maybe you should just talk to her because you're losing your mind and thinking about robbing a bank. Then you could go back to hating her after she helps you."

Jason shook his head. "I can't. I've been so high and mighty about her bad decisions for the past few months. I haven't given her an ounce of grace. I can't exactly admit to this mistake. And like I said, I hate her."

Alita came out of the house, saw Zoe, and scowled.

"Fun's over," Zoe muttered. "By the way, how was your game?"

"Terrible. Mattanawcook killed us, and it was the worst game of my career."

Chapter 14

Esther

Esther nearly fell off the couch in shock when Jason followed Zoe into her apartment. "Jason! Welcome!" She recognized how exuberant her hospitality was and tried to tone it down a notch. "Have a seat!" She got off the couch to make room for them. The three of them would have fit, but it would have been pretty cozy. Looking sheepish, Jason went for the couch. "Would you like anything to eat or drink?"

Jason shook his head without looking at her.

"Do you want some water at least?" Zoe asked.

Jason shook his head again. "Sorry to intrude, but I asked Zoe to bring me here because I could use some advice."

With some difficulty Esther dragged the wooden table chair onto the carpet so she could sit and face them. "I'll be happy to help if I can."

"You might not be able to. I'm not sure what I'm expecting you to say. I don't see a miraculous way out of this." He took a deep breath.

Esther could easily imagine a miraculous way out of this, but she bit her tongue. For now. She eyed Jason. He didn't look like himself. Had he lost weight? There were bags under his eyes, and his hair was disheveled, though that could have been from basketball practice. "Jason, I only know a little bit about what's going on, but I can promise you that God still has you. He is still in control of this, and he still has a plan, so even though it feels impossible, try to relax and trust him."

Jason's eyes filled with tears, and he averted his eyes toward the dark window.

"So I got my friend Chevon pregnant. I can't even believe that I did that, but I did. My girlfriend doesn't know. And I don't want her to find out. But she probably will find out if Chevon has a baby." He chuckled humorlessly. "And Chevon doesn't want to have a baby, but I don't know if I want her to have an abortion. And she can't even have an abortion unless I give her a thousand dollars, which I don't have." He gasped for air. "I'm sorry to disappoint you. And the first thing you're going to tell me is that abortion isn't an option. But maybe that's what I need to hear." He looked at Esther expectantly.

"That's not the first thing I'm going to tell you. The first thing I'm going to tell you is to forget about Alita."

His eyes widened. "What?"

"Are you in love with Alita?"

He looked bashful.

"Do you love her?"

He shrugged. "Seems like we've been together for most of our lives. She says we're going to get married someday."

"I don't care what she says. I'm asking you if you love her."

"I don't know."

"And do you love Chevon?"

His lips curled up in the briefest of smiles but then fell again. "I don't know."

"Well, do you know that your voice sounds completely different when talking about these two young women?"

He shook his head.

"I'm not telling you that you shouldn't love Alita. But I don't think you do. And whether you do or not, she is the least of your worries right now."

"But if I break up with her, everyone might find out that I cheated on her."

"So?"

Jason's eyes widened. "So? So everyone will think I'm a creep!"

Esther leaned closer to the boy. "Jason, you need to stop thinking about what other people think of you. All that matters is what God thinks of you."

His facial expression suggested that this was brand-new news to him. "I don't want everyone to think I'm a cheater."

"Well, I'm sorry about that. But trust me, it is the least of your worries."

He closed his eyes.

"You kind of *are* a cheater," Zoe said matter-of-factly.

Esther looked at her sharply, but Jason chuckled.

"Doesn't mean I want everybody to know it."

"You are going to be known for lots of things in this life, Jason," Esther said. "Most of them good, a few of them not so good. Don't worry about it. One day you will have a family, and it will matter what they think of you, but other than that, truly, God is your only judge."

Jason nodded. "I guess I could convince my brain of that. But I'm not sure the rest of me will buy it."

"You asked for my advice. You don't have to follow it. But step one according to Esther is to break up with Alita. Would you like to hear step two?"

He pressed his lips into a thin line and then exhaled dramatically. "I don't know."

"Tell me how you feel about Chevon."

"We've been friends a long time. She's great. I never really thought of her in that way, but ..."

"But?"

"But there is something about her. I mean, I do care. It's weird. I care more now because I got her into this mess."

Esther gave him several seconds to continue, but he didn't. "So how do you feel toward her now? I'm not asking about love. What else do you feel toward her? Admiration, disgust, frustration ..."

He shrugged. "I like her. She's a cool person. I care about what happens to her ... I guess I'm feeling kind of protective of her."

"Have you said any of this to her?"

He shook his head. "I think she hates me."

"I don't think she hates you."

He leveled a gaze at her. "No, I think she really might. You should hear her talk about me. She called me a cocky narcissist."

Zoe laughed, and Esther tried to scold her with her eyes.

"What else does she say?"

"I dunno, but she's not really big on saying nice things to me."

"Maybe she figures you get enough of that from other people," Zoe muttered.

Esther was thankful when Jason completely ignored this snide comment.

"All she ever says to me is, 'Where's the thousand dollars?'" He sounded so sad—almost like a boy who loved a girl who didn't love him back.

Or maybe that was just Esther *wanting* him to be in love with this girl. "And why is it going to cost a thousand dollars?"

Jason shrugged. "I guess that's the going rate." He looked out the window again and added, "She says her parents would pay for it if she told them, but she doesn't want to tell them ... for obvious reasons."

Suddenly, Esther wished Cathy were there. She was so much better with talking. And then she wished Rachel were there. Rachel was good in a crisis. Suddenly she wished all her friends were there, crammed into her small apartment dealing with this alongside her. "Has she done anything to suggest that she's having doubts about having an abortion?"

"No. I think she's got her mind made up. She wants this over, and I'm seriously considering drastic measures to come up with that money. Legal or illegal, if I thought of a good plan, I would've done it already."

Esther's heart raced. She tried to appear calm when she felt anything but. "I don't think that will be necessary. Are you sure you don't want any snacks? I have found food helps me think."

Jason shook his head, but Zoe said, "Do we have any pie?"

"No, but I've got some fresh cookies on the counter. Bring them on over."

Zoe jumped up and was in the kitchen in four strides. She returned with a cooling rack of cookies, which she set on the coffee table. Esther grabbed one and hoped there was wisdom in the raisins. She knew the question she had to ask, but she really didn't want to ask it. "Do you think she'd let me talk to her?"

Jason looked down at his hands. "I don't think so."

"What's her last name?"

"Sherman."

Esther took a bite of her cookie and then thought as she chewed. Sherman sounded familiar. "Do you know her parents' names?"

"Mary and Phil."

"Wow, rattled those right off," Zoe said.

Jason glanced at her. "I've known her since seventh grade."

"Seventh? Why not kindergarten?"

"Chevon moved here in seventh grade."

Darn. Transplants. She probably didn't know the family. "Oh, wait! I think I do know Mary Sherman. I think I have met her before. She used to do Tupperware. Or maybe she still does."

"I have no idea," Jason said. "But no, I don't see how I could get her to talk to you. She'd probably kill me if she knew I told anyone." His eyes slid to Zoe again. "Though apparently she tells people because that's how I got here."

"It's a good thing you are here, even if you can't see that yet. Could you invite her to church?"

She expected him to reject this idea immediately, but he didn't. He chewed on his lip. "I guess it can't hurt to try."

"Tell her the church will give her a thousand dollars," Zoe said.

"Will you stop with the church and money?" Jason said.

Zoe looked offended. "I wasn't saying that the church *would* give her money. I was just saying to say that they would."

"Let's not entice her with lies. Let's just invite her and let the Lord entice her."

Chapter 15

Chevon

Chevon had no desire to go to church, but she wanted to get out of the house. She was excited that Jason was finally paying some attention to her, even if he had only invited her to church. His unwillingness to deal with this problem had her beyond frustrated. What had she expected, though? This was Jason DeGrave. He'd gone the first sixteen years of his life without a problem, so now that he had one, he was frozen with indecision and inaction. She wanted to punch him.

He pulled into her driveway and got out of the car. She hurried toward the door so he wouldn't have to interact with her parents. Not that they suspected anything—they didn't, but still.

"Where are you going?" her mother asked.

She did not want to tell her that she was going to church. "For a drive with Jason."

"Just Jason? Where's Alita?"

"I think we're picking her up," she lied.

Her mom came to her and gave her a hug. Let me go, Chevon thought, before Jason gets to the door. Her mom did let her go, and she practically flew out of the house, almost smashing into Jason on her steps.

"What's your hurry?"

"I'm really excited about Jesus," she said as sarcastically as she could.

He followed her to the car and started to get the door for her, which he'd never done before.

She looked up at him. "What are you doing?"

"I don't know," he said sheepishly. "Just trying to be nice."

"Well, stop it. My mom is probably watching out the window."

"Fine." He walked away, his shoulders slumped.

Chevon rolled her eyes. "Oh, will you stop sulking? I'm the one who's knocked up."

His eyes widened in horror as he got into the car. She got in too and grinned at him. Seeing Jason panicking made her feel better about her own panicking.

"Why don't you say that a little louder?"

She looked at the house. "Oh, for crying out loud, we're fifty feet away, and there's a wall between us."

He started the car. "Thanks for coming."

"I had nothing else to do and I had to get out of that house."

"Why? Do they know?"

"No, of course not. But I feel like it shows, even though it doesn't. I'm scared they're going to figure it out. And they've definitely noticed that I haven't been acting like myself."

"Oh. Good. I mean, not good you haven't been acting like yourself. Anyway, I think you'll like church." He sounded as if he didn't believe this, but she appreciated his effort.

"We'll see."

He stayed quiet for a few minutes and then, sounding nervous and awkward, asked, "How are you feeling?"

"What do you mean? I'm still feeling like I'm having a twenty-four-seven panic attack. How about you?"

"No, I mean how you feeling with the baby? Are you sick?" He glanced at her, and she was amused at how nervous he was. She couldn't remember ever seeing Jason nervous. "Does it hurt? Are you tired or anything?"

She shrugged. "I'm exhausted, but I think that's because I don't sleep anymore."

"But you're not sick?"

She shook her head. "Nope. But my boobs hurt."

His face got as red as a lobster, and her satisfaction was so complete that it almost made it all worthwhile. She giggled. "You asked."

"You're trying to embarrass me."

"Maybe," she said playfully. She definitely was, but she wasn't about to admit it.

He slowed down as he approached the church.

"Wow, there's a lot of people here." A sudden nervousness swam over her.

"Quite a few, but don't worry. Just stick with me."

He almost sounded protective of her, and she liked it. She shook her head to help herself focus. She couldn't go getting all gaga over Jason. He had enough of that from the other girls. "Hey, before we go in. I don't want to harass you, but how you coming with the money?"

He looked irritated, and this infuriated her.

"Hey, sorry to bother you with this but you did get me pregnant."

"I know that. You don't have to keep telling me. But I don't have the money yet."

"You know, we do have a time limit on this thing—"

"I know!" he snapped. He looked up at the church. "Come on, Let's go in."

She got out of the car, now having strong doubts about this whole church thing. He slowed down and waited for her. Then they walked up the steps together. When she got to the top, she stopped. What had she been thinking? This was stupid. "Jason, I don't think I can do this. I'm sorry."

He took her hand. "Come on, Chevon. I got you."

Despite her commitment to not having feelings for the guy, her heart softened. She allowed herself to be led through the giant wooden doorway and into a small foyer where a woman in an Easter egg purple dress and a giant orange hat greeted them with an enthusiasm Chevon found alarming.

"Good morning, Rachel." Jason dropped Chevon's hand but then put his hand on the small of her back. "This is my good friend Chevon."

Rachel shook her hand. "Welcome, Chevon. What a pretty name!"

Chevon grimaced. She hated her name. Always had. Her mother always said it was a name fit for an Irish princess, but then her parents had mangled the spelling so that people thought she was named after goat meat.

"Welcome to New Beginnings!" the woman said dramatically.

It registered for the first time what the name of the church was. New Beginnings. What an odd name for a church. But she liked it. She wished she could have a new beginning. "Thank you," she managed.

Rachel opened a second large wooden door for her, and Jason led her inside. Her eyes swept the place. It was a beautiful giant old room, like the hall of the castle. A humongous organ sat in the corner with a tiny woman playing it. Dozens of people bustled about. So this was what church looked like. It wasn't quite what she'd pictured. It was louder, happier, and had fewer scarves.

Jason gave her a moment to let it all soak in, and then his hand was on her back again. "Come on. I usually sit over here."

Chevon followed him but was soon stopped by a little girl in her path. Because she didn't know what else to say, she said, "Hi there."

"Hi!" the little girl chirped. "You're really pretty."

Chevon's cheeks got hot. "Thank you."

"Would you like a doughnut?"

Chevon did want a doughnut. She wanted two doughnuts, but she was too shy to say so. "No, thank you. And you're really pretty too."

The little girl grinned mischievously and ran away.

Chevon looked up at Jason.

"That's Judith. She's a Puddy. They're very friendly."

Chevon didn't know what a Puddy was but didn't care enough to ask. She let herself be led to a pew and sat down. Though there was a cushion on the seat, it didn't do much cushioning. "Now what?"

"Now we just relax. The service will start in a few minutes. You don't have to do anything. We just sit here."

That was a relief.

An older woman approached with a giant smile on her face. "Good morning, Jason!"

"Good morning, Esther."

"This must be Chevon?"

Chevon froze. How did this woman know her name? She looked at Jason in a panic. Why had he told an old woman at church? Did that mean that everybody at church knew? She looked around wildly. No one else was looking at her, but this woman was sure suspicious. Esther reached out for her hand, which Chevon gave.

"Yes, this is Chevon. Chevon, this is Esther, Zoe's grandmother."

"Welcome, welcome. Let us know if there's anything we can do for you." She gave Jason another smile and left.

Chevon looked at Jason. She felt like she was on fire. "Does that woman know?"

"What? Why would you think that?"

"How did she know my name?"

"Because I told her that I was inviting you."

"Oh." Chevon faced front as breath rushed out of her. Okay. That did make some sense. Zoe was like Jason's bestie, so it was somewhat logical that her grandmother would be excited to see him bring a friend. Don't be such a freak, she told herself. Not everyone is out to get you.

Chapter 16

Esther

Esther was going up and down the rows, picking up trash and putting hymnals back into their pew-back racks when Zoe said, "Um ... Gramma?"

Esther looked up. "What is it?"

Zoe was staring at her phone. "Something bad's happened."

Esther made a beeline for her. "What is it?" she said quickly.

Zoe looked at her with wide eyes and then looked around the sanctuary as if looking for someone.

"Zoe! What is it?" Esther tried to look at the phone.

"Did Jason and Chevon already leave?"

Esther sighed. "Yes, they sprinted out of here like their pants were on fire." She hadn't even gotten a chance to talk to the girl.

"Maybe we should try to get them back."

"Zoe!" Esther snapped. "What is it?"

Zoe held the phone out so that Esther could see. Esther squinted, trying to make sense of what she was looking at, but the text was too small.

"Chevon's friend got drunk last night and told everybody."

"Told everybody what?" Esther said even though she knew the answer to that question.

"Everything. Everyone knows everything."

"Oh no," Esther said. She reached for a pew, found one, and sank into it.

"Yes. A really big oh no."

A million thoughts raced through Esther's mind. "There's one good thing to come of this."

"What's that?"

Esther turned to face the sanctuary and held her hands up around her mouth. "Rachel, Cathy, Barbara, Vicky, Vera, Dawn! I need you in the upper room, stat!" She saw Walter look at her curiously from a few feet away. "And Walter!" she called out.

Zoe reached for her sleeve. "Are you sure?"

"I'm not sure about anything these days. Come on, you're invited too." She followed the charge for the stairs. Vera paused to let everybody else go first, and Esther felt guilty for making the meeting upstairs. They probably could've done it in the corner of the sanctuary.

They barely fit in the upper room and took their time getting arranged as they waited for Vera to catch up. Esther ended up standing, the top of her hair brushing against the slanted ceiling on the side of the room. As soon as Vera walked in, Walter said, "What is it, Esther?"

Esther took a deep breath. "One of our youth is dealing with something serious, and I'm not sure how to help him. So I thought I would ask all of you for help."

All eyes in the room went to Zoe.

"No!" Zoe held up both hands. "It's not me!"

"It's Jason," Esther said.

"Jason?" Vicky cried. "What's wrong with Jason?"

Though she was in no danger of being overheard, Esther lowered her voice anyway. "The young woman who was at church

with him today is Chevon Sherman. She is a junior in high school."
Esther looked at Zoe. "That's right, right?"

Zoe nodded.

"And she is pregnant."

A few women gasped, but mostly they were silent.

Vicky broke the silence as she was wont to do. "And?"

"And what?" Dawn said. "A pregnant teen is going to need our help."

"It's a bit more complicated than that," Esther said. "I wanted to talk to her, but I didn't get a chance before she left, but I think Chevon is planning on terminating her pregnancy."

There were more gasps this time.

After a short hesitation, Barbara said, "Well, we have to stop her."

"Obviously, Barbara." Dawn looked at Esther. "What are her parents saying? Are they going to let her do such a selfish thing?"

Esther had no idea. She looked at Zoe, who looked at her phone.

"I don't know if her parents know yet," Zoe mumbled.

"A lot of people know, though," Esther said, "so I don't think she'll be able to keep it from them. So maybe they'll take care of the whole thing. Let's pray they do. And then I think we should be ready to spring into action and support this new baby."

"And what if they don't?" Barbara said.

"What if who doesn't what?" Esther said.

"What if they don't do the right thing? What if her parents want her to get an abortion?"

"Then there's probably not much we can do," Walter said.

Barbara's face twisted into a grotesque expression of horror. Esther wasn't sure if the horror was directed at the situation or at Walter's comment. "We can't just do nothing!" Barbara cried indignantly. "We can't just let her have an abortion!"

Walter chuckled dryly. "I don't think we'd be able to stop her."

"Why are you laughing?" Barbara cried. Esther couldn't remember seeing her so wound up.

"We could at least try talking to her," Dawn said. "Tell her what the Bible says about murder."

"I don't think talking to her is going to do much," Barbara said. "Do you really think a teenage girl is going to listen to a bunch of old biddies?"

"Then what do you suggest, Barbara?" Dawn asked.

Esther looked to Cathy for help, but she appeared to be deep in thought. "Cathy? What do you think?"

"Not sure yet. Someone talking to her might help, but I don't think it should be all of us. That would scare the tar out of her."

"She should be scared!" Barbara said. "If she's considering what you're saying she's considering, she should be very scared!"

"Of course she's scared!" Rachel roared. It was the first time she'd spoken, and she was red with fury. "How could you think anything else?" Her back was ramrod straight, her hands curled into tight fists. "And you should all be scared too, sitting here in the house of God, talking about a young woman like this! She is in *need*! We need to love her, not call her a murderer!"

"But she's thinking about being a murderer!" Barbara said.

"No, she's not!" Rachel cried. Her whole body trembled. "She's not thinking about anything of the sort. In her terrified little heart, she doesn't know that it's murder. She sees that she has a major problem that's going to change her life forever. She probably thinks she's not capable of being a mother. All she sees is the problem, and she sees only one way out of it."

"A selfish way," Barbara said.

"Barbara!" Rachel barked. "You need to stop talking right now!"

Esther's heart skipped. Her friends had endured disagreements before, but Rachel and Barbara were *really* angry right now. It was scary. Maybe she shouldn't have called them all together into this tiny room.

"Maybe we should all just take a break," Walter said holding his hands out.

Esther wasn't thrilled that the only man in the room had just told a bunch of women to calm down, but she was glad *someone* was trying to diffuse the situation.

Vicky, however, didn't think they needed his help. "We've been having arguments for several decades, *Mr.* Rainwater." She emphasized the *Mr.* in front of his name. "I don't think we need you to referee us."

Walter folded his arms across his chest and backed up against the wall.

"We need to know where her parents are at before we know how to move," Cathy said slowly.

"Agreed," Rachel said. "This is a family matter."

"Are you saying we don't do anything?" Barbara cried.

"She said no such thing," Vicky said. "But what are *you* saying exactly, Barbara? What are you saying we should do? Do you want us to tie her up in the church basement and keep her healthy till she gives birth?"

It was ridiculous, but Barbara's facial expression suggested she hadn't been thinking of anything much different.

Cathy looked at Zoe. "I'm not asking you to be nosy, Zoe. But is there any way you can find out where her parents are at?"

Zoe nodded soberly. "I think so."

"Thank you. Then I guess for now we adjourn, and we all pray without ceasing."

"Good plan," Rachel said. "But I think we should all pray about it right now together."

"All right." Cathy looked at her as if waiting for her to start.

Rachel nodded at her. "Go ahead."

Cathy chuckled and bowed her head. "Father, we asked you to give us people to minister to, and you have answered that prayer. We're not sure what to do here, so lead us. Give us wisdom and grace. We pray for this young woman, we pray for the child, and we pray for Jason. Please let each of them feel your comfort, your peace, and your strength. We ask you to bless them with good health and with courage. In Jesus' name we pray. Amen."

Chapter 17

Chevon

Despite the fact that Jason was still an annoying jock who had no answers for her, Chevon was in a better mood when he dropped her off than she'd been when he'd picked her up. She hoped this was the effect of going to church and not the effect of just being around Jason for a few hours. She knew she had some weird feelings for him, but she told herself they were only hormonal and would go away when the pregnancy went away.

Her good mood faded as she went up the front steps to her house. A foreboding settled in her stomach. She had a feeling that something bad was going to happen, which was stupid because something bad had already happened, and now she was home, and home was a safe place.

The house was quiet, and she closed the door behind her wondering why.

"Chevon?" her mom called. "We're in the living room."

Did that mean that they wanted her to join them? Her dread deepened. They knew. She didn't know how they knew, but they knew. She forced her feet to carry her to the living room. Her dad stood with his elbow resting on the mantelpiece, his face as red as fire. Her mom sat on the couch and patted the seat beside her. "Come, sit, honey."

Chevon didn't want to sit but she knew it wouldn't do any good to run away. She sat.

"I don't know which part of this makes me the angriest," her father said evenly.

"Phil! Let's not start off with the anger." Her mom looked at her. "We love you, we're here for you, and we will help. We're a little overwhelmed, as I'm sure you can understand. But what matters is that you know that we love you, we are here for you, and we will help. But first we need to ask if it's even true."

Chevon burst into tears and buried her face in her mother's chest. Her mom wrapped her arms around her and squeezed. She kissed her on the top of her head. "Oh, honey, I wish you had told us. How long have you been carrying this around all alone?"

Chevon shook her head. She'd lost track. "A few weeks," she mumbled.

"And Jason DeGrave is the father?" her father asked.

Chevon sat up and wiped her eyes, nodding.

"How long have you been sleeping with Jason DeGrave?" He said his name with hatred.

"Phil!" her mother scolded.

"What?" he barked. "I didn't even know she was sexually active! Pardon my shock to find out she's sleeping with some other girl's boyfriend!"

"I thought you liked Jason," Chevon muttered.

"I don't anymore! Answer my question!"

Chevon had forgotten what the question was. She looked at her mother for help.

"I asked how long you've been sleeping with him."

"I only did it once," Chevon cried. She had never wanted to rewind her life so badly. She wished she could go back to that night and run like the wind. She wished she could never see Jason DeGrave again. She wished she'd never met him.

"You only did it once with him or you only did it once?"

"Phil! Would you please take it easy? This is your daughter!"

"Is it? I'm not so sure!"

"Phil! Stop!" Her mother took both her hands into her own. "First thing tomorrow morning, I will call to make you an appointment. I will go with you. It's not a big deal. It doesn't even hurt. Everything will be back to normal soon."

Her father guffawed. "Back to normal? Everyone in town knows that she slept with somebody else's boyfriend. Do you know what they're saying about her?"

Despite her suffocating guilt, Chevon rolled her eyes. "Dad, everybody sleeps with everybody. The rumors are the least of my worries."

"Oh, how nice for you!" he screamed. "Well, they're certainly concerning to me! I seem to be the only one who cares about this family's reputation!"

It wasn't that she didn't care about the family's reputation, but it was pretty far down on her list of priorities.

He started out of the room. "Don't leave this house, but I need a break. It's hard for me to look at you right now."

Chevon watched him go. She couldn't believe it. She'd known that he would be angry, but she hadn't known he was capable of this kind of anger. This was all going worse than she'd ever imagined. But at least now she would get the help she needed. This was a tremendous relief. And then she could get on with her life. She sniffed. "Will I miss any basketball?"

"No." Her mom rubbed her knee. "You sure won't. Anything I can do for you, honey? Do you want some lunch?"

She *was* hungry, but she was desperate to get into her bedroom and shut the door. She shook her head. "I just want to go to my room."

"Okay, go ahead. But please, I am here for you. Please don't shut me out."

"Thank you, Mom."

Chevon dragged herself up her stairs and into her bedroom, shut the door, and collapsed on her bed facedown. Sobs exploded out of her, and she let them come until she was all emptied out. Then she thought of Jason. Did the whole town really know? If so, how? And while she didn't really care about what people said, she knew the opposite was true of Jason. She sat up, a new panic in her gut, and pulled her phone out of her pocket.

She texted him, "Everybody knows."

He answered immediately. "I know."

He texted again. "My phone is blowing up."

"I'm sorry," she wrote even though she didn't know if she was the one who had leaked it. "But we can chill now. My mom will make an appointment. Don't worry. You're off the hook. It's all over."

Chapter 18

Jason

Jason had kept his phone on silent throughout the church service, so by the time he checked it on the way out of Chevon's driveway, he had three missed calls from Alita. As he stared at her name on his screen, his stomach turned with dread, and then the phone was silently ringing again, her name across the screen larger now, accusing him. As he debated whether to answer, he noticed he'd also missed multiple texts. He declined the call and opened the first one.

It was from Hype. "Why am I literally always the last person in town to know anything? Give me a call."

The next one was from Alita. "CALL ME RIGHT NOW" in all caps. Not wanting to read the others, he turned his phone off. What was he going to do? Where was he going to go?

If Hype was right and everyone in town knew, then it would only be minutes before his parents found out, if they didn't know already. He couldn't go home. So he kept driving but then he passed two seniors walking down the street and they both stared at him as he drove by. He had to get out of this town. He glanced down at his gas gauge. No way. He might be able to get to Bucksport, but he couldn't get back. That might not be so bad, but he didn't know how much help it would be to be stuck in Bucksport.

He drove to the boat landing and parked. He shut the engine off to save gas but then two minutes later started it again. It was too cold to sit there with no heat.

Whether he drove or whether he idled, his gas wasn't going to last forever. He had to come up with a plan. Maybe he should just go hang out with Esther and Zoe. They were pretty safe, and they would feed him and not shame him. Maybe they'd even let him move in. He turned his phone back on to ask Zoe if she was still at church or if she'd gone home, planning to hint for an invitation, but as soon as his phone turned on, it buzzed with an incoming message from Chevon. "Everybody knows."

No kidding. And how had that happened? How many people had she told? He shook his head. He didn't want to be mad at Chevon of all people. This was all his fault. "I know," he typed. "My phone is blowing up."

"I'm sorry. But we can chill now. My mom will make an appointment. Don't worry. You're off the hook. It's all over."

Jason's head swam with this new information. It was going to be over. Relief washed over him. But that relief did not last long. Because a new fear took hold. What if Esther was right? What if this was a horrible crime they were going to commit? A crime against God? Was he really going to let Chevon do that? And if he decided that he didn't want to let her do that, how could he even stop her? How could he go against her and her parents? He didn't think he could. So was he supposed to sit back and let it happen? He didn't know. Would God hold him accountable for something they did?

A new question popped into his mind that made tears roll down his cheeks. Would that baby hold him accountable? Would that little child of his wonder why her daddy hadn't protected her? Or him? This thought was too much to bear. He wiped at his cheeks and put the car in reverse. As he turned around, he texted Zoe, "Are you guys still at church?"

"Yes. You okay?"

"Yes."

"Can you talk? I'll call."

He put the car in park again. "No need. I already know that everybody knows."

"Okay. Sorry. I didn't want to be the one to tell you."

"I appreciate that."

"Do you know if her parents know yet?"

"They sure do. I'll be right there." As he sent the last message, Alita called again, so he turned his phone off again. He knew he was being a jerk by not facing her, but he just couldn't right now. Esther had been right. Alita was the least of his worries.

Jason drove back to the church and parked in front of it. As he got out, he wondered if they didn't want him to park there. They probably didn't want their church associated with him. But with no place to hide the car, he left it where it was and went inside.

Zoe met him at the door. She looked like she wanted to hug him, but she didn't.

Jason scanned the room. Most of the ladies were still there chatting. "Where's Pastor?"

"He had a meeting," Esther said.

Jason didn't know if that was good or bad. He desperately needed help, but he didn't really want to admit to the man what was going on. One of the women came toward him. He didn't know her well, but he was pretty sure her name was Barbara. "What are her parents planning to do?"

Jason looked at Zoe, who looked at the floor.

"Sorry. I told them that her parents know."

"It's okay." He sighed. And it was okay. There were no more secrets, and that was the only positive he had right now. "They're going to get an appointment for an abortion."

"So that's it?" Barbara cried. "They're not going to think about other options?"

Jason took a step back. "I have no idea."

"Well, maybe you should be over there with them instead of here!" Barbara nearly shouted.

Jason decided he didn't like Barbara very much.

"Stop it, Barb," Vicky said. "Cut the guy some slack, and I'd bet my hat that her parents don't want him anywhere near that place right now." She looked at Jason. "Have a seat. We were just praying for you. You can join us."

Jason sat and put his head in his hands. Esther sat behind him and lay a warm hand on his back. He looked up at her. "What am I going to do?"

"I have no idea. I think, for now, you are going to do as Vicky says and pray along with the rest of us."

"Actually," a male voice said, and Jason looked up to see Roderick standing near the doorway. "Could I have a minute alone with Jason? Then you guys can have him back for prayer."

Jason followed Mr. Puddy into the basement nervously. He hardly knew this man, so what was this about? Was he going to give him some man-to-man advice? Scold him? Preach at him?

"Have a seat." Roderick flicked on the lights. "This won't take long." He sat down facing Jason and rested his elbows on the folding table. "Don't worry, I'm not going to preach at you."

Jason laughed. Good.

"I just want to tell you something that I've learned. It's not even advice. It's only my experience, and you can take it or leave it."

Jason nodded.

"Jason, I've done some pretty cool things in my life. I've had some fun, I've had some adventures, I've traveled a bit, and I'm telling you that there is nothing as rewarding and gratifying and wonderful as having babies."

Jason blinked. He hadn't known what to expect, but this certainly wasn't it.

"I can't even tell you how much fun it is having a family. I was skeptical at first, a little nervous when the woman I love first got pregnant, thinking children were going to be a huge expense and tie me down."

Jason nodded. He fully understood this part of the conversation.

"But they don't tie me down. Instead, they cut my strings, and now my spirit soars every day with the joy of them. And they're not an expense. Children are wealth. Children are more valuable than any dollar you will ever earn or ever spend. They are more fun than college scholarships, diving saves, home runs, or buzzer-beating threes. They are more fun than women fawning over you and your name in lights." He paused and leaned forward a little. "You do what you think God wants you to do, but I just wanted you to know that you have an opportunity here for infinite blessings and joy. If you want to take God up on this offer that he's giving you right now, then know that you are in for years and years of rich, rewarding life. And I think that's the way God intended for us men to live. You know the whole be fruitful and multiply thing? Yeah, I think he was talking to us."

Chapter 19

Rachel

Rachel sank into her couch and kicked her shoes off. Hearing of Chevon's plight had plunged her headfirst into her own past. Her memories now so sharp and vivid, she was back in that maelstrom of emotion: shame, confusion, disappointment, and crippling fear. She remembered that fear was so powerful she'd thought it would kill her before she could decide what to do.

And she'd been an adult! She couldn't imagine what it must be like to go through this at sixteen or seventeen. Things had changed a lot since then. Maybe Chevon wasn't experiencing the shame and guilt that Rachel had gone through. No. Things might have changed, but somehow Rachel knew that Chevon wasn't escaping that part of the package.

Rachel lay down and stretched out. She couldn't believe how awful her friends had been. Barbara and Dawn had talked about Chevon like she was a monster. What would they think if they knew how close Rachel had come to aborting her own daughter? Esther had been reasonable, thank goodness. And Vicky had been unusually quiet. What was up with that? Rachel would have thought she would have been the most judgmental of all. Thank God for small favors.

What had they been thinking? That they were going to have some sort of intervention and bully the girl into keeping the baby? Not only was that insane, but it wouldn't even work.

Rachel closed her eyes. Should she go talk to her? She sort of had the inside scoop. But she couldn't do that. She didn't even know this girl. It wasn't like it had been with Zoe. She couldn't trust this girl with her biggest secret. What were the chances she'd keep it? More likely she'd be annoyed and tell the first person she saw. And then what were the chances that Rachel's daughter would find out the truth? Pretty good, Rachel feared. And she couldn't let that happen. So no, she wasn't meant to talk to this girl. It wasn't her turn this time.

"Father ..." She took a deep breath. "It seems all I can do is pray. I pray you help Chevon make the right decision. If you want us to help, show us how. Please use me while still allowing me to protect my daughter, like you always have."

Chapter 20

Zoe

On Monday morning Zoe found Levi leaning on her locker with his hands in his pockets. When he saw her approaching, he stood up straight and smiled his lopsided smile.

"Good morning," he said.

"Morning. You're here early." Levi was usually late.

"Yeah, I wanted to talk to you. Wanted to catch you before there were a ton of people around." He shifted his weight to his bad foot and then quickly back again and shoved his hands deeper into his pockets until his elbows were ramrod straight.

She opened her locker. "Oh yeah? What's up?"

"I ... eh ... wanted to ask you out on a real date this weekend."

She froze. Her brain worked a mile a minute as her mouth hung open, waiting for words that her brain wasn't delivering. Finally, because she didn't know what to say, she said, "I'm sorry, but I can't think about that right now. I've got too much going on."

His face fell. "You mean you've got too much Jason going on."

"I didn't say that."

"You didn't have to. I thought maybe his impending fatherhood would make you less in love with him. But I guess I was wrong."

"I'm not in love with him."

"If you say so. But for the record, I wish you had just said no. So the next time some guy gets up the nerve to ask you out, give him the honor of just saying no." He stared at her for a few seconds and then turned and walked away.

She felt horrible, but she wasn't sure how she could have handled that moment differently. She didn't want to go out with Levi, and he had caught her off guard. She hadn't been prepared. She'd expected to never be asked out in her life, let alone by Levi in the school hallway this morning.

Maybe he was right. Maybe she should've just said no. But she hadn't wanted to hurt his feelings. And she hadn't been lying. She *was* completely consumed by Jason's problem and couldn't think about anything else. She'd spent practically the whole day before at the church praying about it and she'd lost sleep last night thinking about it.

Jason came up to her. "You okay?"

"Yeah, why?"

Jason shrugged and looked in the direction Levi had walked. "I dunno. Levi was just acting weird and now you look like you're about to throw up."

"Yeah, I don't feel so good." She slammed her locker.

"Do you want to go home?" His furrowed brow made her feel a little better. He was actually concerned.

"Nah, I think it will pass."

"Okay. Let me know if you change your mind. I can give you a ride."

"Thank you."

He headed toward their first class even though it wouldn't start for another fifteen minutes, and she fell into step beside him.

People stared at them as they walked by, whispering and giggling. "Sorry about that," Zoe said quietly.

"Yeah." Jason took a deep breath and exhaled slowly. "Me too. I hate it. I wish I didn't hate it as much as I do."

"I've been the subject of rumors for a long time if you'd like any pointers."

He laughed genuinely. "Yeah, sure. Go ahead."

She hadn't expected him to say that. She couldn't come up with any pointers. "Don't make eye contact with anyone," she blurted out, "and skip school as much as possible."

He laughed again. "That's terrible advice."

"Yeah. That's kind of my specialty."

They walked into the classroom and sat down. Jason took his phone out and started fiddling with it, so Zoe followed suit as the rest of their classmates trickled in. She kept an eye on the door, watching for Chevon, curious how she'd be acting—but Chevon never entered the room.

During announcements Zoe whispered to Jason, "Is Chevon coming today?"

Jason shook his head. "I thought so."

"Is today the day?"

Jason looked at her, obviously annoyed. "Is today what day?"

She gave him an are-you-serious look. "Is her appointment today?" she whispered.

"Shhh!" His shushing was far louder than her whisper had been and garnered more attention from their classmates.

"Listen to announcements please," the teacher said.

Jason waited for the attention to die down a bit before saying, "I don't know when it is. Her mom was supposed to call this morning."

The teacher gave them another glare, so Zoe stopped questioning him.

But when they still hadn't seen Chevon at lunchtime, she brought it up again. "Haven't you texted her?"

Jason nodded.

She waited for him to say more. "And?"

"And she's not telling me much. She just says not to worry, that it will all be over soon."

"She didn't tell you when the appointment was?"

"No." Jason slowed his chewing.

This was weird. Wouldn't Chevon want Jason to go with her? If it were Zoe, she would want him to be there. "Well ... did you ask?"

With difficulty he swallowed. "Of course I asked. She told me not to worry about it."

"Not worry about it? It's your baby! Of course you're going to worry about it." Instantly, Zoe felt guilty for using the word baby. Was it a baby? Everybody at church certainly acted like it was. But she still wasn't sure. Then out of nowhere, she thought of Rachel's story. She closed her eyes, trying to remember clearly. Hadn't Rachel said that her daughter had been an unwanted pregnancy? Yes, but more than unwanted. If she was remembering right, Rachel had gotten pregnant because of rape. Zoe dropped her fork, and it rattled loudly when it hit the table.

"What?"

"Nothing."

"It's not nothing. You just thought of something." Jason looked over his right shoulder. "What, did you just see Levi staring at you?"

She looked at Levi and sure enough, he was looking at her, but he looked away quickly when their eyes met. "No, I didn't know that, but thanks for pointing it out."

"So what is it?"

"Nothing." But it was something. She just couldn't tell him yet. She had promised Rachel she wouldn't tell anyone and then she'd mostly forgotten about the whole thing because she had so much going on in her own life and she'd been drunk and stoned when Rachel had told her. The memory itself was foggy, but she was pretty sure she remembered the main points. So Rachel needed to talk to Chevon. Zoe was surprised that she hadn't already done that. But she'd left church long before the others yesterday. So maybe she didn't know all the developments.

Zoe needed to talk to Rachel.

Jason interrupted this train of thought with, "So, what happened with Levi?"

Zoe quickly looked down at her food. "Nothing."

"You know he likes you, right?"

She raised her eyes to meet his. "I don't know that."

Jason laughed humorlessly. "Oh, come on. It's so obvious."

Zoe didn't like this conversation. She certainly didn't like having it with Jason. And she didn't like thinking about Levi liking her. It scared her to death, and it made her feel overwhelmingly guilty. She had handled this morning so poorly. Why had she been so dumb? She hadn't meant to hurt Levi's feelings and felt sick that she had.

"You don't like him?"

How could Jason be so dense? Didn't he know that she was in love with *him*? Although, as she had this thought, she wondered, *am* I love with him anymore? Suddenly, she wasn't so sure. She still cared about him a great deal but as she sat there staring at him, she realized she wasn't quite as smitten as she used to be. In fact, she was pretty annoyed. "I don't know."

"Well, I think you should give him a chance."

Zoe rolled her eyes. "You barely know the guy."

"I know him well enough to know he's okay. But I said that because he's the only guy in the school taller than you."

Zoe looked at Levi quickly. "He's not taller than me!"

Jason laughed. "Maybe not right this second, but once his ankle heals and he can stand up straight, he will be." Jason gave her a smug look that made her want to slap him.

All through practice, Zoe thought about Levi. She didn't think that she liked him, but she didn't understand why turning him down had made her feel so bad and so guilty. She was annoyed with herself for ruminating on it. She needed to let it go, but she couldn't.

Finally, when she stepped into her grandmother's apartment, she was able to distract herself again with Jason. "I need to talk to Rachel."

"Okay. Hello to you too. Want some dinner?"

"Could you invite her over?"

Gramma laughed uncomfortably. "Is everything okay?"

"Yes. I think she could help Chevon."

Gramma furrowed her brow. "Oh? Why is that?"

Zoe hesitated. She'd spilled way too many secrets lately. "Because she helped me when I was in trouble, so I think she should talk to Chevon."

It was clear that Gramma accepted this explanation. "Okay sure. I'll give her a jingle."

Chapter 21

Rachel

Rachel's spidey sense started tingling as soon as Esther issued her invitation. It was practically the middle of the night. Why did Esther want her to come over in the dark on a Monday night? She could think of no good, safe explanation. She hadn't had a peaceful moment since she'd found out that young lady was pregnant, and she feared God was about to ask her to share her secret yet again, but she didn't want to. But now an invitation to Esther's sounded like God was about to push the issue.

She couldn't even get herself excited about Esther's food because she'd already eaten her supper. Because it was the middle of the night.

Still, she couldn't exactly decline the invitation, so she made the short drive to Esther's apartment building. Esther welcomed her warmly into her small home and didn't act as if she'd suddenly learned some giant dark secret about her old friend. But Zoe wouldn't take her eyes off Rachel. So it was Zoe who had cooked up this little plan. Oh boy.

Esther tried to engage in pleasant small talk, but Rachel wasn't in the mood. She hadn't gotten much sleep the night before and she was near desperate to get home and into her jammies. Rachel leveled a gaze at Zoe. "So, what can I do for you ladies?"

Zoe took a deep breath and said, "I was hoping you would talk to Chevon."

Rachel glanced at Esther, trying to gauge how much she knew, but Esther looked clueless.

"I thought we had decided that it wasn't time for that yet?" Rachel asked, trying to stall. She didn't want to answer the question that Zoe was really asking. She didn't even want to hear it.

"We did," Esther said, "but then the young woman came to church, and now we've learned that her parents do in fact know. Sad to say, the whole town knows, so now these kids' struggle is very public, which isn't going to help anything. And now we know that her parents are in favor of terminating the pregnancy." She glanced at Zoe. "Zoe thought, because you were able to help her, that you might be able to help Chevon."

Rachel relaxed a little. She'd been right in thinking Zoe had kept her secret. Or maybe she didn't even remember it! She had been a little sauced that night when Rachel had opened up to her. "I talked to you, Zoe, because I clearly felt God nudging me to do so. I don't have that leading this time." This was almost a lie. Rachel wasn't sure whether there was any nudging because she was working so hard to avoid it.

Zoe's face fell. "Okay."

Rachel thought that was going to be it, but then Zoe looked at Esther and said, "I'm sorry, Gramma. Could I have a moment alone with Rachel?"

Rachel's stomach rolled.

Looking confused, Esther said, "Sure. I'll go for a walk."

"Don't go for a walk!" Rachel said. "It's the middle of the night and it's freezing outside!"

"I wasn't going to go outside, silly. I'll just go see who's in the common room. I'll be back in five." Her words were polite, but her tone suggested that this conversation indeed had a five-minute limit to it.

This was good. Rachel hoped Zoe would talk fast. They watched Esther leave, and then Rachel turned to look at Zoe, her eyebrows raised.

Zoe took another big breath. "I was thinking about what you told me. About your daughter."

Rachel's chest tightened in panic. She didn't want to think about this, let alone discuss it. And she certainly wasn't going to consider sharing something that private with a complete stranger. Again she couldn't believe that she'd done it for Zoe. Maybe she shouldn't have. Because it had brought her to this place. "What I told you was incredibly private, and I can't tell anyone else because my daughter can never find out."

Zoe nodded quickly. "I know that, but I don't think Chevon would tell anyone."

Rachel folded her arms across her chest. "I'm surprised to see you this dedicated to the cause."

Zoe's eyes fell. "I don't know what I'm dedicated to. I don't even know what I want. I don't know what's right or wrong in this situation. But I just feel bad for Chevon, and I don't want her to do something that she's going to regret later."

"What would you do if you were in her situation?"

Zoe laughed humorlessly. "That's ridiculous."

"Answer the question."

"I don't know."

"Answer the question, Zoe."

"Wow, Rachel, are you trying to teach me a lesson? Fine, I won't ever invite you over again."

Rachel tried to soften her voice. "No, Zoe. Please, answer the question."

"What does it matter?"

Rachel wasn't even sure, but she thought that it did. "I just want to know."

"If I had been in your shoes? I would've had an abortion. No doubt. But if I was pregnant with Jason's baby right now?" She laughed again to show how preposterous the hypothetical situation was. "I would probably want to keep the baby because it's part of Jason."

"And you love Jason."

"I don't know. I'm not so sure that I do now."

This was great news. The girl was growing up, getting healthier. "So do you think Chevon should keep the baby because it's part of Jason?"

Zoe looked at the ceiling. "For the millionth time, I don't know. I certainly can't imagine raising a baby at sixteen. I can barely take care of myself." She blew her bangs out of her face. "All of this is above my pay grade. I think I just want them both to be safe and happy."

"Both? The baby and Jason?"

"I meant Jason and Chevon. Yeah, I guess I mean the baby too."

Rachel really didn't want to do this, but she could practically feel God's hand on her back pushing her toward it.

She had to talk to Chevon. And that meant something else. That meant she was going to have to tell her daughter because she couldn't take the chance of having her daughter finding out some other way. The idea made her feel weak, and she sat on the couch.

"All right. I'm not making any promises about what I'll say to her, but if you can get me alone with Chevon, I'll talk to her."

Chapter 22

Zoe

There was a weird bounce in Zoe's step on Tuesday morning. She still didn't know what her role in this whole mess was supposed to be, but for the first time she thought she was on the right path. All day she looked for an opportunity to get Chevon alone, but there were always people around.

Finally, she saw her opportunity in the locker room before practice. "Hey, Chevon!" She tried to sound cheerful and friendly, but neither of those things came naturally to her. Chevon looked up and looked terrified. Zoe had never been mean to her, of course, but she'd never spoken to her either. And Chevon had probably been harassed a bit in the last few days. Zoe gave her a big smile, but the fear on Chevon's face intensified, so Zoe thought maybe the smile was scarier than not smiling and dropped it. "I have a weird idea," she said quickly. "If you don't want to, that's totally cool. I won't be upset or anything. I have this friend ..." Shoot. Should she have called Rachel her friend? Was that weird? "She's an old lady, but she's also my friend. She's been a big help to me. She's just really good to talk to, and I thought maybe you'd like to talk to her."

Chevon just stared at her. "And it's not your grandma?"

Zoe laughed awkwardly. "Gramma's also great to talk to, but no, this is Rachel. You'll probably recognize her from church."

"The one with the hat?"

Zoe laughed again. "Yeah, that's her. Don't let the hats scare you off."

"Hats? As in plural ... there's more than one?"

"Oh, there's so many more than one."

Coach Hodges stuck her head through the door and told them to hurry up.

"Coming!" Chevon called.

"I thought maybe we could go after practice, if you're up for it."

"My parents want me to come straight home after practice." She sounded sad.

"Oh, okay." That did make sense. Zoe was about to drop it when she had another idea. "You want to ditch practice?"

Chevon laughed. "Are you serious?"

"Sure, why not?"

"Because I've never ditched anything in my life."

"Oh, wow. You are really missing out." Zoe felt a little guilty leading a good girl to the dark side. Then she remembered that this good girl was pregnant and didn't feel so bad. It looked like she was considering it, so Zoe gave her a minute. "We're already late anyway. Might as well be even later—"

"You know what? Let's do it. I don't even really want to talk to her, but I really, really don't want to go to practice, and this sounds like a good enough reason not to."

"Okay." Zoe grabbed her backpack before Chevon could change her mind and headed toward the outer door.

"Aren't you going to change?"

"No way. Ditchers have to act fast."

"Okay then." Chevon giggled as she ripped off her sneakers and slid her feet into the shoes she wore to school. She shoved her sneakers into her locker, slammed it shut, grabbed her two giant bags, and hurried after Zoe.

Zoe got the door for her, feeling tremendously accomplished that she was pulling off such a stunt.

Once they were outside and on their way to Chevon's car, Zoe asked, "I thought you liked basketball?"

"I did three days ago, but now my teammates are all treating me like I've got the plague." She pointed her fob at the car and the locks clicked.

Zoe opened the door. "Oh, it's nothing like the plague. I hear it's not even contagious."

Chevon laughed, and Zoe wondered why they hadn't been friends before. And as soon as she asked herself the question, she knew the answer. She'd been so busy following Jason around that she hadn't even tried to make other friends.

Chevon backed out of her parking spot and then stomped on the accelerator, throwing Zoe back into her seat.

"Wow, you sure were in a hurry to get out of there."

"I so was, and I didn't even realize it till you mentioned it. I hate that place. I hate everyone." She looked at Zoe. "Wait, were you joking about ditching?"

Zoe wasn't sure. "No, not at all. I ditch things all the time. It's sort of my superpower."

Chevon giggled again, and it brought Zoe genuine joy. She'd been picturing Chevon in some deep dark depression about all of this, but right now the girl sounded happy.

"Okay, where does she live?"

"I have no idea."

"Wow, you guys are really close friends."

Zoe laughed. "Shut up." She took out her phone and called Gramma. "What is Rachel's address?"

"Why, are you mailing her something?"

"No, Chevon and I are on the way there."

Gramma gasped. "Oh my! Good job, Zoe!"

Zoe flinched, hoping Chevon couldn't hear Gramma's voice.

"I don't know Rachel's address off the top of my head."

"Can you just tell me where she lives?" It was a small peninsula. Zoe thought she could figure it out.

"Yes, she lives right beside where the Ference Hardware Store used to be, in the purple house."

"I have no idea what the Ference Hardware Store used to be."

"I do," Chevon said.

"Okay, Gramma. Thank you." Zoe hung up and looked at Chevon, who had started driving again. "Why do you know where an old hardware store is? I thought you were one of the few people who haven't lived here forever."

"I haven't, but there's a giant old wooden sign on the side of the building that says Ference Hardware Store."

Zoe laughed. "Wow, you're quite the detective."

Chapter 23

Jason

Alita climbed into his car, eyes red, eye makeup smudged. She slammed his door. "Are we going somewhere?"

He'd asked her to meet him at his car. He hadn't said they were leaving the school parking lot. "No. I just wanted to talk somewhere private."

"Well, drive somewhere," she ordered. "I'm not sure if I want to be seen with you." She looked toward the doors of the school.

This surprised Jason. Normally Alita thrived on drama. The more spectators the better. He started the car but didn't take it out of park. "This isn't going to take long. I know you hate me, but I had to say that I was sorry."

"You wait till the end of the day to speak to me and then you say this isn't going to take long? Wow, thanks for penciling me in!"

He suppressed a groan.

"You know what the worst part is?" She returned her attention to the front doors of the school.

That he had cheated on her with one of her friends? He didn't answer her.

"That I had to hear about it from some loser's text message. Are you kidding me? Why couldn't you just tell me?"

He thought the answer to that was pretty obvious, so he didn't give it.

"Did you actually think you were going to get away with it? In Carver Harbor? Nobody ever gets away with anything!"

He leaned back against the headrest. He was tired. He wanted to get this over with. "I'm not asking you to forgive me, but I just had to say that I was sorry. And that's pretty much it."

Her head snapped in his direction, and there was fire in her eyes. "That's it?" she screeched. "Are you serious?"

"I don't know what else you want me to say."

"We were supposed to be together forever. We are supposed to get married."

"I know," he said quietly. "I'm sorry."

"Stop saying you're sorry!" she screamed.

He opened his mouth to say he was sorry but then snapped it shut just in time.

"I don't want to hear how sorry you are. I want to hear how you're going to fix it!"

Fix it? What did that mean? How did she want him to fix it?

"Well? Are you going to say anything?"

"I'm not sure what you want me to say."

"Stop saying that!" she screamed. "I want you to say that you're going to help her get rid of this stupid pregnancy and then you're never going to look at or speak to her again. I want complete shunning. Then we can try to get back to normal. And I want you to say that you're never going to cheat on me ever, ever, ever again!"

He was gobsmacked. He hadn't expected any of this. "Alita," he said, trying to be gentle, "I don't think we can survive this."

"Of course we can," she snapped as if he were a stupid child. "Just let me take care of that."

He shuddered to think of how Alita would be treating Chevon in the future. Whether or not he ended up with Chevon, he couldn't stay with Alita and allow Alita to try to ruin Chevon's life. All of a sudden, he was too tired to be dealing with this anymore. He just wanted her out of his car. He knew that was wrong, but he didn't care.

Through clenched teeth, she said, "I can find you the money, if that's the holdup."

He felt sick. He was going to pretend he'd never heard those words. "We need to break up."

"No!" A torrent of curses came out of her mouth at a piercingly high pitch. "That is not the way this is going to end! You don't get to break up with me!"

"I'm not breaking up with you. You're breaking up with me because I'm the jerk who cheated."

"Jerk?" She snickered evilly. "I think that's the understatement of the century."

"Call me whatever you want. I'm sorry for being dishonest, and I'm sorry that I hurt you. But this relationship needs to end, and this conversation needs to end."

Her mouth fell open, and her whole body shook with rage. "You're sorry for being dishonest? Does that mean you're not sorry that you slept with Chevon?"

He opened his mouth to say that he was sorry for that too, but the words didn't come out. Was he sorry? Sometimes, yes. But sometimes he wasn't. He didn't know. It was too confusing, but it felt like if he told Alita that he was sorry he'd slept with Chevon, then that would be betraying Chevon in some way. "Alita," he said, again trying to be gentle. "Please get out of my car."

At first she made no sound and no movement. But then she wailed. Just a crazy, long high-pitched wail. Then she opened the door and as she got out of his car, she screamed, "I hate you so much!" She slammed the door and then whirled toward the building to check the doors.

Chapter 24

Chevon

Crazy Hat Lady's house was almost the same color purple as her dress had been on Sunday. It looked like the world's biggest Easter egg.

Chevon followed Zoe into the house and was amused to see that the first room they stepped into sported walls of the brightest yellow she'd ever seen.

"Welcome! Welcome!" Rachel said and ushered them into the living room, where the walls were orange. Chevon looked around the room in wonder. Walls and tables were adorned with framed pictures of children dancing, posing, and swinging bats.

Zoe started to slip her shoes off, but Rachel stopped her. "No, no. Keep your shoes on. I don't want your toes to get cold."

Zoe looked down at the floor. "I don't want to get your carpet dirty."

Chevon looked down as well and smiled when she saw the bright blue of the carpet. She could see why Zoe had been concerned; the carpet looked brand-new.

"Nonsense. Your comfort comes first. Have a seat, ladies. Can I get you anything to drink?"

Zoe declined the offer, so then Chevon felt guilty doing otherwise.

Rachel sat in an armchair and turned her body to face them. She looked directly into Chevon's eyes. "So, tell me the truth. How are you doing?"

Her sincere concern brought on a flood of tears. Chevon wiped them away quickly. "I'm okay, I guess."

"No offense, honey, but there's no way you're okay."

Chevon shrugged. "I guess I feel better now that my parents know. I was really scared."

Rachel hesitated. "Scared of what?"

That was kind of a stupid question. "Scared that I was pregnant."

"Obviously. But what specifically about it scared you?"

"I was scared that people were going to find out. I normally don't really care what people think of me, but this one was big enough that I did care. I was scared about getting fat. I was scared about having my body ripped apart. Not going to college. Not being able to afford the abortion. Scared of disappointing my parents. Scared the abortion would hurt." She stopped. She thought there were probably more things, but she couldn't think of them right now.

Rachel had listened intently to her list and now she nodded thoughtfully. "That's a lot to be scared of. I'm so sorry you're going through all of this."

Chevon looked down at her hands. "Thank you, but I did it to myself."

"You weren't alone. Tell me about Jason."

Chevon looked at Zoe nervously. She knew Zoe was in love with Jason and wasn't sure she wanted to discuss her feelings—or lack thereof—in front of her. Of course, Chevon knew nothing would ever happen between Jason and Zoe, but still.

"Go ahead," Zoe said. "I don't care anymore."

Chevon wasn't sure what that meant, but she found she didn't really care. She took a deep breath. "What do you want to know about him?"

Rachel tipped her head to the side. "I think you know. I want to know what you think about him. How do you feel about him?"

Again Chevon was far too aware of Zoe's presence beside her, but Zoe seemed clueless as to the effect she was having on her. "We've been friends since I first moved here. Pretty good friends actually. Me, him, and Hype do a lot of stuff together. He's a good guy. A really good guy. He annoys me a lot, but I would do anything for him. And he really is good. I care about him a lot, I guess. I didn't think I cared enough about him to have his child, but ..." She'd meant it as a joke but then couldn't bring herself to laugh. She was too worn out.

Rachel laughed gently. "Did you want to have sex with him?"

Chevon got so hot so fast she worried she was going to start sweating. Did this woman really just ask that? She glanced at Zoe out of the corner of her eye, but Zoe only sat there like a log.

"I'm sorry, dear. Sometimes I'm too frank. I am asking if he pressured you into it or forced you."

Chevon shook her head emphatically. "Oh no, nothing like that." She let out a long sigh. Did she really want to admit all of this? To herself, let alone to others? She looked at Zoe. "If you tell anyone any of this, I will literally kill you."

Zoe smirked. "Mum's the word."

Chevon turned to Rachel. "I didn't think that I liked him. I didn't want to be his girlfriend or anything, but lately I have been getting a little bit jealous of Alita. And so it was actually my fault. I mean, of course he was excited about it and everything, but I sort of initiated it." She rubbed the back of her hand across her forehead, trying to keep the sweat under control. "Part of it was that I was mad at Alita, which is so embarrassing." She forced herself to look at Rachel, whose expression was gentle and understanding. "Really, I don't know what I was doing. It just sort of happened. I sort of wanted it to happen. I don't know why."

"And now?"

"Now what?"

"Have your feelings for him changed?"

Chevon looked down at her hands. She didn't want to admit this. "Maybe. I don't know. Everything is mixed up inside, and he's kind of been a big doofus ever since I told him I was pregnant."

Rachel tipped her head back and laughed at the ceiling. "That sounds about right. He is a man, after all."

Oddly, Rachel's joke made Chevon feel defensive of Jason. "I mean, I guess if I had to choose between being with him and not being with him, I would give it a try, but I also won't die if he doesn't choose me." No one said anything. "If that makes sense," she added. "And I don't think he wants to choose me."

"I wouldn't be so sure," Zoe said.

Chevon looked at her sharply. "What? Did he say something to you?"

"He said lots of stuff to me, and I *really* don't want to get in the middle of it. I'm just saying I think he might be willing to give it a try too. But that's just my opinion. I'm not quoting him."

Something sparked in Chevon's heart. A weird little jolt of energy. But then her racing thoughts took over, and the jolt faded. "I don't know what it matters. I don't know if our friendship will survive this, let alone anything more."

Rachel looked at her curiously. "Why do you think your friendship might not survive this?"

She shrugged again. "It's so awkward. He's always going to know what I've done. Every time he looks at me, he's going to see his mistake. He's going to associate me with the abortion."

"Chevon, I ask you this without an ounce of judgment. Are you sure you want to have an abortion?"

Chevon nodded quickly. "Absolutely. I'm sixteen."

Rachel nodded. "Okay. I'm not going to tell you what to do—"

Beside her, Zoe snickered.

Chevon looked at her. "What's so funny?"

"Sorry, I just wasn't expecting that. Rachel likes to tell *me* what to do."

Rachel gave Zoe a sobering look, and the smile slid off Zoe's face.

"Like I said, I'm not going to tell you what to do. I just want to tell you *my* story. Would that be okay?"

Chevon nodded. She wasn't sure if she wanted to hear it or not, but she was in the woman's house, so she couldn't exactly say no.

Rachel got up, crossed the room, and took a picture frame off the wall. She brought it back and held it out in front of Chevon. It was an old picture of a baby. "This is my daughter, Hope." Just as Chevon was wondering if she was supposed to take the photo from her, Rachel whisked it away. She went to a different wall and took down two more photos, which she brought back. She held one out for Chevon to see. "This is Hope when she was seventeen." The picture showed a beautiful girl with big hair holding a soccer ball. She showed her the third picture. "This is Hope with three of my grandchildren. Tucker, Mackenzie, and Keith." She gave Chevon a few seconds to admire the photograph of the happy strangers and then she sat down again, still holding the picture frames.

She looked down at the picture of her grandchildren. "I don't have words to explain how vitally important these four humans are to this world." She looked at Chevon. "You can't imagine yet how much you will one day love your child, whether it's this one or another one. So just take my word for it. There is no feeling more pleasant, more satisfying, more joyful than the love I have for my child, and the love I have for my grandchildren. Each of them is an individual who makes the whole universe worthwhile. Times that power by four, and that's why I don't have the words for it."

Chevon's body tightened. The woman might not be going to tell her what to do, but Chevon could see where the conversation was heading. She braced herself. Just wait for her to stop talking and then say you don't feel well, she told herself.

"I wasn't as young as you, but I was young. I was alone in the world, and I had no idea how to be a mother. I got myself into a scary situation, and someone took advantage of me."

A sick feeling washed over Chevon. She'd been wrong. She hadn't known where this conversation was going.

"I'll spare you the details, but I'm sure you can imagine. I was beyond terrified. I had been violated, I was ashamed, and I had no one to turn to." She leveled her gaze at Chevon, and Chevon felt as though she was looking inside of her. "I had a choice to make. There weren't as many options back then, and services were harder to get. In this day and age I really don't know what I would've done, but back then, I chose to have my daughter." Her eyes grew wet with tears. "And it was so obviously the right decision. One of the best I've ever made. The amazing, mighty, beautiful woman who is Hope wouldn't exist if I had made a different decision. My grandchildren Tucker, Mackenzie, and Keith wouldn't exist if I had made a different decision. I wouldn't have met my husband and I wouldn't have my other children. Now of course, I would've had a whole different life, and I might've had different children, but there's no way that life would have been as fulfilling as the one I have." She leaned closer to Chevon and softened her voice. "I tell you my story only so that you might feel less alone. I am always here for you." She glanced at Zoe. "Zoe's grandmother is always here for you. We will help you with this every step of the way, no matter which route you choose. We are here to love you and support you and help you."

Chevon couldn't believe what she was hearing. These people were strangers to her! Her own mother hadn't offered this level of support. No one had. Not even Jason.

Rachel leaned back in her chair. "I can read your mind."

Chevon doubted that as she could barely read her own thoughts, they were so jumbled.

"You're thinking we're all going to die before this baby becomes a toddler."

The thought of her pregnancy as a toddler was completely foreign to her and took her by surprise. No, she had never considered that the cells inside of her could ever become a toddler. She barely knew what a toddler was. And yet she was picturing one right now. A little girl looking up at her. The startling image had chubby cheeks and a giant smile.

Rachel laughed joyously. "And you might be right. But it doesn't matter because what I'm telling you is that the church will help you. And I don't mean the building you went to on Sunday. I don't even mean the people in that building. I mean the whole church. Every believer in the world makes up one big church. We call this church the body of Christ because the people are his representatives on earth. Don't flinch"—Had she flinched? She wasn't sure.—"I'm not going to get all religious on you. I only want to make this one point. The body of Christ will be here for you for the rest of your life. And if you choose to have this baby, we will be here for him or her for the rest of his or her life. I will be dead and gone eventually, but you will have Zoe. You will have Jason. You will have believers you haven't even met yet. So don't think that you can't handle this. You can because you will have help." She snapped her mouth shut. "That is all I wanted to say."

Chapter 25

Chevon

Chevon could barely drag herself out of bed on Wednesday morning. She knew that her mom would let her stay home from school, but she needed to talk to Jason. Besides, as much as she didn't want to go to school, holing up in her bedroom all day would drive her even closer to crazy.

She was on her way to her car when she had a better idea and felt stupid for not thinking of it sooner. She went back up her steps as she texted Jason, "Can I hitch a ride?"

Her mom looked up when she walked back in. "Something wrong with your car?"

"No. I think I'm just going to ride with Jason."

Her mom looked suspicious. "Why's that?"

"I want to talk to him."

"About what?"

Chevon stared at her mother. "Are you serious?"

"Really? You want to talk about your unplanned pregnancy on the way to school? Won't that get you in an emotional upheaval?"

"I have been in an emotional upheaval every second since the first day my period was late."

Her mom frowned. "You know what I mean. Won't it get you even further shook up?"

"I don't see how that's possible."

Her mom stepped closer. "I don't know if I've told you. I've talked so much the last few days and it's kind of a blur, but I'm really impressed with how levelheaded you're being about all of this. You're being very mature." As she reached out for her, Chevon was annoyed, but when she pulled her in for a hug, Chevon relished the familiar feel of her arms around her.

Her phone dinged, and Chevon pulled away to check it. It was Jason. "Sure."

"Thanks," she texted back. She looked up at her mother. "He'll be here in a minute."

Her mother studied her. "I'm not sure it's a good idea to be spending more time with him."

"I'm not planning on sleeping with him again," Chevon said dryly.

"I'm glad to hear that, but I'm not sure he's a good influence."

It had been her fault just as much as it had been his, but she wasn't about to tell her mother that. "He's probably the best-behaved boy in town."

Her mom raised an eyebrow. "I guess we have different definitions of well behaved."

Chevon waited for her to tell her that she wasn't allowed to ride to school with him. She knew she was thinking about it. But her mother didn't say that. "I love you. Have a good day. Stay levelheaded." She went back into the kitchen, and Chevon turned to face the window to watch for Jason.

When he pulled in a few minutes later, Chevon groaned. Zoe was in the car. Of course. Chevon had forgotten that Jason gave her a ride too. So much for being able to talk to him before school. She went outside, trying not to be annoyed with Zoe. Zoe was being a good friend to her, and Chevon didn't have many right now. But now Zoe was hogging the front seat, and Chevon was going to have to climb in the back, which was stupid because she had her own car.

Sure enough, as soon as she shut the door, Jason asked, "Car trouble?"

"Yeah," she said because she didn't want to say, "No, I wanted to talk to you about my feelings" in front of Zoe. Frustrated and annoyed, she stayed silent all the way to school. At least he was no longer giving Alita a ride.

Jason caught her eye on the way across the parking lot. "Are you okay?" he mouthed.

She nodded. "Need to talk to you," she muttered.

"Okay. Soon."

Nevertheless, he didn't make himself available throughout the day, and by lunchtime she found herself seriously jealous of Zoe. Not long ago she'd been jealous of Alita. Now she was jealous of Zoe? She had to get a grip. She looked at their lunch table. Jason, Zoe, and Hype. There was room. She could join them. But everyone would notice that. She never sat with them because she usually sat with her female friends. But her female friends weren't acting like friends anymore. Oh whatever, she thought. People were talking about her already. Like sitting with him was going to amplify the gossip that much. She headed that way, surprised at her nervousness.

Hype grinned when she got there. He spread his arms out. "Welcome to the cool club!"

Jason looked surprised and even maybe a little displeased with her arrival, but it was too late now. She sat down and picked up her fork, even though she had no appetite.

Hype looked at Jason and then at Zoe, who had gone noticeably silent. "So, how's your day going?" he asked Chevon.

"Not great. I don't really have good days anymore."

"Sorry to hear that," Hype said and sounded as if he meant it. "Hear you girls ditched practice yesterday. What a bunch of rebels."

Jason looked up. "You did?" He sounded horrified.

Chevon nodded, feeling a little proud. "My teammates are being obnoxious." This made her wonder: if she decided to keep the baby, would she have to quit basketball? Part of her found this idea devastating. Part of her didn't care. She felt Zoe looking at her and met her gaze. "Thanks for that, by the way."

Zoe didn't respond.

Chevon got the feeling that Zoe didn't appreciate Chevon being in her territory. So much for that new friendship. Chevon didn't want to sit there like a zombie, so she forced herself to eat. She couldn't taste anything, and it was hard to swallow. She was grateful that Hype was distracting everyone by making fun of their science teacher.

Chevon hoped that Jason would linger a bit when lunch was over, since she had told him that she needed to talk to him. But when the period ended, he jumped up like he'd been absolutely desperate for that bell to ring and vanished into the crowd. She looked at Zoe, but Zoe ignored her and wordlessly left the table too. Chevon felt tears come to her eyes and tried to bite them back. She wasn't going to cry alone at the lunch table. She had plenty of reasons to cry, but Zoe being rude to her was not one of them.

Chapter 26

Rachel

"Mom? What's going on?" Hope said. The worry etched on her face made Rachel feel guilty. She sat down quickly.

"I'm sorry, honey. I didn't mean to scare you." Rachel looked around the restaurant to see if anybody was within earshot. She scooted her chair closer to the table, closer to her oldest child. "It's not bad news." But wasn't it? Wouldn't it be bad news to Hope? Rachel fought the swelling in her throat. She looked down at the menu. "Let's order first. Then I'll explain."

"Mom, no. The suspense is killing me. What is it?"

But the server was approaching, so Hope looked up at her, and her face transformed into a polite smile. The women ordered their drinks, and the server left again.

The smile fled Hope's face, and she looked at her mother sternly. "Spill it. Now."

Rachel nodded. But the words didn't come. This was absurd as she had been practicing for hours.

"Mom, you're scaring me. Spit it out."

"Just give me a second. This is really hard for me. I have to tell you about something..." The tears came then fast and hard whether Rachel wanted them to or not.

Hope reached across the table and took her hand. "Oh my gosh, Mom, what is it? Are you sick?"

"No." She swallowed hard and took a deep breath. "Recently I had the opportunity to help a teen who is in trouble."

Hope's face relaxed a little, and she nodded. "Okay."

"This teen is pregnant and wondering if she should have an abortion."

Hope's face relaxed even more. "Oh. Okay."

"And you know how God wants us to use our own experiences to help others."

Hope nodded. "Mom, if you had an abortion, you don't have to tell me."

Rachel reeled back. "Of course I haven't!"

"Oh, okay. Sorry."

Rachel hurried to explain, not wanting to leave her confused. "But the truth is, I did think about aborting you, and I'm so, so sorry—"

Hope held up one hand. "Stop."

Rachel stopped. "What?"

"You don't have to do this."

"No, I do. Let me finish. It will make sense in a minute."

"No, it already makes sense." Tears sprang to Hope's eyes and rolled down her cheeks. "You don't have to do this because I already know the story."

Rachel frowned. "What?" What story? She certainly didn't know the one Rachel was about to tell unless Zoe had called her.

Hope squeezed her hand. "Mom, I love you so much. Thank you for wanting to tell me, but Dad already did."

"What?" Surprise and anger surged through Rachel. But he had sworn to her that he wouldn't! "He did *what*?"

Hope grinned through her tears. "Go easy on him. He did it out of love. He told me not to tell you because he knew you didn't want me to know. But he said he couldn't go stand before his Father in heaven with a lie between him and his daughter."

Tears gushed out of Rachel's eyes remembering her husband's integrity, his giant heart. She nodded, unable to speak.

"He told me what happened and I'm so, so sorry that you had to go through that, Mom. But he is my father in every sense of the word, and if anything, the facts of history teach me that he was more my father than he would have been if he was my biological father. Because he *chose* me. He chose to be my father and that means more than any biological contribution ever could." She squeezed her hand again. "So thank you for finding me a father like that."

Rachel unwrapped her silverware and used the scratchy napkin to try to get her tears under control. She knew they were wreaking havoc on her mascara and foundation. She swallowed hard. "Hope, I love you so much."

"Mom, I know you do. I've never doubted it for a second, and when Dad shared your secret with me, my understanding of what love means changed completely. That kind of love can only come from God, and I thank you for letting him love through you. Thank you for giving me love every second of my life, even when I was being knit together in your womb." She picked up her own napkin and wiped at her eyes. Then she smiled at her mother. "Thank you for giving me life."

Chapter 27

Chevon

"Well, well," Coach Hodges said after the girls' team had lined up on the baseline. "What an honor it is to have you two join us." She was looking at Chevon.

She was noticeably *not* looking at Zoe, and Chevon realized that she, being the experienced athlete, was going to take the brunt of the blame for skipping yesterday. Coach Hodges must've been the only woman in town who didn't know Chevon's secret. No, obviously the athletic director didn't know either, or she wouldn't be playing. Or maybe they both knew but pretended not to. Chevon was pretty good. Maybe they didn't want the team to have to play without her.

"You guys missed some conditioning yesterday, so today we're going to do some extra to make up for it!"

Chevon's teammates groaned, and one of them swore at her. She was inclined to swear back, but she didn't have the energy.

"Down and back twice!" Coach blew her whistle, and the team took off. Chevon started but then stopped. She wasn't even sure why.

Coach glared at her. "You better start running."

Chevon watched her teammates sprinting down the floor. Suddenly this all seemed so stupid. She loved basketball, but right now she couldn't stomach it. She looked at her coach. "I'm sorry. I just can't." And then she turned and walked toward the locker room.

"Don't you dare walk off this court!" Coach Hodges shouted.

Tears slid down her cheeks, but she didn't stop or turn around.

"If you leave here, you don't get to come back."

Chevon knew that already, and though the idea made her sad, that sadness wasn't enough to make her turn around. She just didn't have the energy. She didn't have the physical energy, but more importantly she didn't have the emotional energy.

The locker room felt cold, and she changed quickly. When she had her coat on, she texted Jason, "Where are you?"

The response came immediately. "Weight room."

Oh great. That place would be packed too. She headed that way, which was awkward because she had to walk through the gym, but the only other option was to walk around the gym outside, and once again, she didn't have the energy for that. She avoided the eyes of her teammates and her coach and trudged up the stairs to the weight room.

When he saw her, he came right to the doorway. "Why aren't you dressed?"

His question annoyed her. That was what he was concerned about? "I am dressed." It was true. She was wearing clothes.

He blinked, confused.

"Got a minute?"

He wiped his sweat off on his sleeve and nodded. She led him out of the weight room and into a corner of the balcony where they wouldn't be seen by the people on the court below. "I'm having lots of crazy ideas. Thought maybe you could help me sort through them."

He nodded eagerly. "Of course."

He was gazing at her so intently, it put butterflies in her stomach. Instinctively, she put her hand on her stomach, and then, worried he might think she was thinking about the baby, she dropped it.

Suddenly she was nervous. She'd wanted to tell him that she was having weird thoughts, crazy ideas, scary doubts. But now she didn't dare tell him any of those things. "I just wanted to check in, I guess. See how you were doing with everything?"

His eyes widened. "You're worried about how I'm doing?"

"Well, not really worried." She grinned. "Just curious what you're thinking."

He hesitated. It looked like he wanted to say something but didn't quite dare. Odd. That's how she was feeling too. "We just haven't talked much you know, since ... in a long time." Maybe ever. They'd spent a lot of time together, but she didn't think she'd ever had a deep conversation with him. She wondered what that would be like. Was Jason DeGrave even capable of deep conversation?

"You want to go somewhere?" he asked. "I mean, I can't right now because I have practice, but maybe tonight? We can just go somewhere and talk?" He seemed really into this idea.

"That would be good." His gaze was making her feel vulnerable, so she looked away. "We've got all of these people telling us what to do and how to do it but it's our lives and I think we should be the ones making the decisions."

His eyes widened. "Are you thinking about changing your mind?"

Shoot. She'd said too much. "Not really. I just want to talk to you about it. Feels kind of stupid to talk to everybody else about it and not you."

"Great. As soon as practice is over, I'll take a quick shower and I'll come pick you up. It'll be about six-thirty?"

She nodded. "Thanks, Jason." She gave him a small smile, feeling shy all of a sudden, and walked away. Great, her mom was going to love this. She didn't dare turn around to check, but she thought she could feel his eyes on her as she walked down the stairs.

Chapter 28

Jason

Jason was a weird combination of nervous, excited, and relieved to be pulling into Chevon's driveway. He didn't really know what this was going to be about, so he felt some trepidation. He didn't want to say or do the wrong thing and offend her or push her away. Yet he was excited about spending time with her and about hearing what she had to say. He was also relieved. He had missed his friend, and he thought that being around her would bring him comfort.

He expected her to come running out of the house when she saw his car, but he rolled to a stop, and the door to her house did not open. No problem, he thought. He shut off the engine and got out of the car to go to the door. His phone dinged, and he stopped to check it.

"Don't come."

What did that mean? Don't come? He was already there. He stepped back. Was he supposed to leave? The disappointment was almost crushing. He glanced at the house and then turned to walk back to his car, sad and embarrassed. He'd started the engine when she came bursting out through her front door with her father right behind her. The porch light didn't offer much illumination, but he looked furious.

He bellowed her name. Yep, *furious*.

She picked up speed and was almost to the car when he came down the steps. She ripped the door open and before she even got in, said, "Drive! Drive!"

Jason was not about to peel out of the man's driveway as he approached. He rolled down his window.

Mr. Sherman grabbed the sill of his window as if he were trying to pull the car closer to him. "Chevon!" he hollered into Jason's face. "Get out of this car!"

Suddenly Jason was feeling less honorable. "Please, Mr. Sherman—"

"Don't you speak to me! Don't you even look at me!" He looked at his daughter. "Get out of that car right now!" He started around the front of the car, toward her window.

Chevon whimpered. "Please, just go."

"Why is he so mad?"

"I don't know, maybe because you impregnated his only daughter."

He banged on her window, and she leaned toward Jason. How much force would it take to shatter that window? He feared they were about to find out. Jason didn't want to roll down her window, but he wanted to speak to the man, so he raised his voice. "I just want to talk to her, sir. I'll bring her right home—"

Mr. Sherman ripped her door open, and she shrieked and leaned even closer to Jason. Her dad grabbed her sleeve and started to pull, and she grabbed Jason's arm.

Jason didn't know what to do. He didn't want to defy this man, but he was worried about her safety at this point. "Sir," he said with no idea what he was going to say next.

Out of nowhere, Chevon's mother appeared behind her husband. She grabbed his other arm and started pulling. "Phil, please. Let her go."

"No!" he roared.

"She said she just wants to talk to him!"

"She doesn't need to talk to him!"

But it was working. He had let go of Chevon and had straightened up. If Jason drove ahead, he could probably get away, but there was no way to drive ahead because his car was pointed right at the house. But if he backed up, he was going to hit her father with the open door. Plus, he didn't even know if driving away was the right thing to do. Should he really be kidnapping this girl from her parents?

"Just drive, please," Chevon said.

"I can't! He's in the way."

Chevon pulled away from him and reached with both arms to pull the door shut. She managed a few inches, but then her father realized what she was doing and ripped it open again.

"Phil, you have to let her go!"

The large man turned on his wife. "Don't make out like I'm trying to hold her prisoner. I'm not locking her in the house. I just don't want her going with *him*. I would think my logic would be obvious!"

"Just pull ahead," Chevon whispered. Hadn't they already been over this? He opened his mouth to say again that he couldn't when she added, "Just a little."

He realized what she meant. He stepped on the gas, and the car jerked ahead six feet. She slammed the door just as her father turned to look at her, obvious shock on his face. He hadn't been expecting that. Her mother grabbed hold of him as Jason cut the wheel to the right and backed around him.

He lunged for the car and slapped the hood with both hands.

"Go!" Chevon cried.

"I'm trying!" Jason didn't think he'd ever been so stressed in his life, and he'd been to jail once. He wondered if this was indeed a kidnapping. He didn't want to go to jail again.

He stopped at the end of her driveway and took a breath.

"Don't stop!" she cried.

He looked at her. "Are you sure? You could just get out and walk back to the house right now."

"He's coming!"

Jason looked in the review. Sure enough, the man was running down the driveway. Jason groaned and pulled out onto the road. "I do not feel good about this. I shouldn't be stealing you from your parents." He purposely avoided the word *kidnapping*.

"You are not stealing me," she said emphatically. "I am not property. They do not own me. I wanted to get in your car, and I have the right to do that."

Jason liked the sound of that, but he wasn't sure it was true. Did a sixteen-year-old have a right to anything? His father certainly didn't think so. "Where are we going?"

"I thought you had a plan."

He sure didn't. "Want to go park at the boat landing?"

She sighed. "That's the first place he'll look. Just find a dirt road and drive down it."

"Okay." He drove until he saw a gravel road and then pulled onto it. "Now what?"

"Now stop."

"In the middle of the road?"

"Sure. We'll see somebody coming if they do."

This was stupid, so he kept driving until he came to a wider patch in the road. Then he pulled over, put the car in park, and leaned his head back. "Wow, that was way more excitement than I wanted."

"You're not alone in that. I've had more excitement the last few weeks than I have ever wanted to have."

Jason's heart ached for her. This was hard on him. But he knew it was even harder on her, probably much harder. And his dad didn't know yet, or he might've been right beside Mr. Sherman, chasing after them.

"I wanted to say that I'm really sorry," she said softly, in a voice he hadn't heard her use before. "I didn't mean to get you into this mess."

He couldn't believe what he was hearing. "You have nothing to be sorry for! And I'm not even sorry that what happened happened!" He hadn't known he felt this way until he said the words. "I mean," he hurried to add, "I'm a little sorry we got pregnant, but I don't regret being with you. That was amazing."

It was dark, but still he thought she was blushing.

"Sorry, I'm not hitting on you. I promise."

"What a relief," she said quickly, her voice thick with sarcasm.

Shoot. Had he offended her?

Chapter 29

Jason

"Are you okay with my decision to get an abortion?"

What? Why was she asking him that? And what was he supposed to say? "I don't know. I think it's your decision."

"That's a cop-out, and you know it."

He smiled in the darkness. He was glad that their changing relationship hadn't interfered with her willingness to be frank. She had always told it like it was, ever since he'd met her in seventh grade. While all the other girls tiptoed around offering him nothing but praise, Chevon had always told the truth. She'd praised him occasionally, but *only* occasionally, and only if he really deserved it.

He thought he knew what he wanted to say, but he wasn't sure he had the right. And he wasn't sure he had the courage. He silently prayed. *Help me. Give me the right words. What do you want?* He had never needed God as much as he did right now, and God had never felt so far away.

"Just say what you're thinking. Don't be such a wuss."

There was that honesty again. "I'm not a wuss."

"Sorry, your highness. Didn't mean to offend." Her words were sarcastic, but her tone was light.

"Are you trying to tick me off so that I'll be more honest?"

"Maybe," she said playfully.

"That's really not necessary. I'll be honest with you. In fact, I promise you right now that for the rest of our lives, I will always be honest with you. But I want to do this right. This is your body we're talking about, so I don't want to step over the lines."

"Jason, I honestly don't think that you can make me do anything, so stop worrying about it. I'm asking for your input. This is your baby too."

Jason hesitated. "Baby?"

"Yeah," she said, sounding wistful. "I can't believe I said that either. That's kind of why I wanted to talk to you. I'm having all sorts of weird thoughts. It might just be the hormones."

"What weird thoughts?"

"You first."

Fine. "I think, if it were entirely up to me"—He took a long breath.—"then I would rather you didn't have an abortion. But I also understand if you choose to have one." The first words had been difficult to speak, but now that he had started, he felt emboldened. He turned his body to face her. "I know you don't think that much of me, but I would be different if I was your boyfriend or even maybe, eventually, your husband. I would be different if I was a father. I think I will be a good father. I've had a good father. I know what it looks like. I know how important it is. So you wouldn't be in this alone. And even if you don't want to be with me, but you want to have the baby, you still wouldn't be in this alone. I would still be a good father." He realized how much he had just said and stopped. "Sorry if that was too much, but you asked."

"It wasn't too much," she said softly, and he realized that she was crying.

He desperately wanted to reach out and wipe away her tears, but he didn't quite dare. "Now, what weird thoughts?"

"Wow." She took a shaky breath. "They don't even really make sense. It's just, at first, all I could think about was making this go away. I was so embarrassed, but the embarrassment is mostly gone. Now I'm just angry at everyone who is staring at me. I mean, what do they care, and why do I care that they care? It's all so, so stupid. So sometimes I just think, what if? What if I had a baby? I don't know if you know this about me, but adoption is out of the question. There's no way I can give up a baby. I couldn't even give up a kitten. My mom killed a mouse in our kitchen once, and I cried for two weeks. So it's going to be all or nothing. And sometimes, not all the time, mind you, but sometimes I think I want *all*. And then other times I think I want nothing. I have no idea what I think."

He laughed stiffly. "That's my exact thought. I have no idea what I think."

She laughed too. "I'm like, should two people who don't know what they think really make the decision to end a life?"

These words surprised him. "Do you think it's a life?" He spoke carefully, not wanting to push her. He genuinely wanted to know what she thought, either way.

"I don't know, but it could be. So if it could be a life, maybe it is already. I mean, does it have a soul? Does it have a personality yet?"

He snickered. "I think it's funny that we keep calling it an it. I mean, it's going to be a little boy. Or a little girl."

"I know. So unreal." She put her hand on her belly. "I definitely don't want a baby, but babies are cool. They're like tiny humans."

He laughed hard at this, and a majority of his tension melted away. "They *are* tiny humans, you goofball."

She joined him in his laughter. "I know that. I don't know why I said that."

"It feels so good to laugh. I haven't laughed in weeks."

"I know, me neither."

They were quiet for a moment, and Jason marveled at how comfortable he was sitting there in silence with her. He didn't think he'd ever had a single second of silence with Alita. Suddenly, he couldn't believe he'd spent so many years with her. What had he been thinking? He looked over at Chevon. He wanted to reach out and take her hand, but he was afraid of how she might react.

"But like, what does that look like?" she asked. "What do we do with a baby?"

"I have no idea. And I'm not sure what your dad would say to that idea."

She laughed humorlessly. "Oh, no way. He'd probably disown me."

This was a lead weight on his shoulders. How had he brought his friend to a place where she had to choose between the baby growing inside her and her own parents? How could anyone make that choice? "I'm sorry."

"For what?"

"For causing this problem between you and your parents."

"Speaking of parents ..."

He could feel her eyes on him.

"You haven't said. How are yours reacting?"

"I don't know how it's possible, but they don't know yet."

"I would say that that is impossible, but my coach is acting like she doesn't know either. I guess some people live with their heads in the sand."

"Did you quit basketball? That's what everybody's saying."

"Don't change the subject. Why haven't you told your parents?"

Because he didn't want to, that's why. "I'm scared to tell my dad. But I probably should, so he doesn't find out from someone else. He lives in Bucksport now, or else I think he would've heard by now. My mom will probably never hear because she's like the village pariah. No one talks to her anymore. Including me."

She slapped the dashboard. "Let's go then."

"Go where?"

"Bucksport. To your dad."

"What?" he cried. Was she nuts?

"If we're thinking about having a baby, we need help. We're not going to get it from my dad."

"You're not going to get it from my dad either!" he cried. His whole body stiffened with terror at the thought of telling his father. "My father might literally murder me."

"You just said your dad was a good dad."

"He is. He's a great dad, but he has big plans for me, and this is going to ruin them."

"I don't think it would ruin them," she said softly, sounding hurt. "I think it would only change them."

"You don't understand. My whole life has been about my athletic career, about playing in college. You don't know how much money he's paid, how much volunteer coaching he's done, the hours he's driven to tournaments, the hours he's spent in bleachers—"

"Okay, I get it." She was angry.

He closed his eyes. He didn't want her to be angry. But he didn't want to face his father either. He had to choose. And he decided he didn't want her to think he was a wuss. "Are you sure you want to be there when I tell him? That might be a little awkward."

"I can stay in the car if you want. But yeah, let's go. First, I'm in the mood for a drive. Second, I'm really in the mood to get out of this town. Third, you need to tell your dad. It's not fair that my dad is hollering at me and your dad's not hollering at you." She giggled.

He didn't think he'd ever noticed how cute her giggle was. He put the car in reverse. "Okay then. Let's give it a whirl."

Chapter 30

Jason

Jason's father looked exhausted, and Jason felt guilty. His father looked at Chevon, gave Jason a concerned look, and then stepped back from the apartment door. "Come on in. Have a seat."

Again Jason had the urge to take Chevon's hand, and again he didn't dare to. He silently scolded himself for his lack of courage. Maybe she was right. Maybe he was a wuss.

He sat down on the couch, and she sat right beside him. He was glad she had sat so close. He couldn't believe how protective he was feeling of her.

His dad sat in his recliner. "What is it, son?"

"First, I want to apologize for bringing Chevon." She gave him a sharp look, so he hurried to explain himself. "I don't want to put you on the spot and make you uncomfortable, but she's the one who gave me the courage to come, so I didn't want to leave her in the car."

His father looked bewildered. "It's below freezing. I'd be pretty disappointed if you left a woman in the car."

He was glad to hear his father call her a woman. That made this whole crazy plan seem that much more doable. Did his father know somehow? Did he know what they were about to tell him? Was that why he'd said the word woman? Probably not. Probably just a coincidence. Or maybe he did think of her as a woman. Maybe he thought of Jason as a man.

"I'm sorry I didn't tell you sooner, but I've been scared to. I don't ever want to disappoint you."

"Son, you can never disappoint me. Now spit it out."

Suddenly, Jason knew that his father was going to be okay with this. He was so certain, he wondered how he had ever thought otherwise. His father loved him. Sure he had great expectations and high standards, but his love was more powerful than those things.

Jason looked at Chevon and then couldn't stand not touching her anymore. He put his arm around her and looked at his father. "Chevon is pregnant." He waited.

For a long time, his father just stared at him. Then he leaned back in his chair. "I'm not really sure what to say."

Jason nodded. "Me neither."

"I didn't realize you two were that close."

"Me neither," Chevon said, and this struck Jason as incredibly funny. As he tried to bite back his laughter, he realized that his father was laughing too, so he let it out. It felt so good to laugh. Gigantic problems seemed so much more livable when he laughed his way through them. He would need to remember that because if he was going to be a father, he was probably going to have more gigantic problems in the near future.

The laughter died down, but they were all still smiling when his father asked, "What's the plan?"

Jason shook his head. "I have no idea." Then he felt guilty for answering the question. Maybe he should have let Chevon do it. He looked at her. "What's the plan?"

"I don't think there is one," she said quietly.

His father looked at him and then back to Chevon. "What do your folks say?"

"They say it's not even up for discussion. They want me to have an abortion."

"What do you want?"

Chevon looked at the floor. "I don't know."

His dad looked at him. "What do you want?"

"Well, I don't really want to be a father at seventeen, but if I have to choose between that and an abortion, I think I choose fatherhood."

"You're not seventeen for another two weeks."

Jason's cheeks got hot. "I know. I was thinking I'd be seventeen when the baby gets here."

His father was quiet for a long time. Then he said, "It does seem that an abortion would be the simplest answer."

Jason's stomach fell. He opened his mouth to argue, but his father wasn't done talking. "But I want you to know that if you choose to have the baby, I'm here for you."

Really?

"Really?" Chevon said.

His father nodded. "Of course. Jason's my son."

Chapter 31

Chevon

When Chevon finally got home on Wednesday night, her parents were in the living room waiting for her. Her mother rushed to the door and hugged her before she could even get her coat off. But her father got up and went to bed without saying a word.

Chevon slept like a dead person—completely and utterly exhausted. She woke up feeling better than she had in days but as she came out of the bathroom, she stopped as fear overtook her. The house was too quiet. What did that mean? She didn't know, but the hairs on the back of her neck were standing up. Trying to talk herself out of her fear, she went into her bedroom to get ready.

Wanting to avoid any sort of confrontation, she waited till the last second to go downstairs.

Her parents were in the living room. "Have a seat," her father said.

"She doesn't have time right now, Phil. She has to eat breakfast and get to school."

"She's not going to school."

Because she didn't know what else to do, she sat on the couch.

"I'll make you some toast." Her mother went to the kitchen.

"I'm sorry about last night. I lost my temper, but I really hate that kid. He violated you, and he's just going to get away with it. You're the one who has to go through the abortion, and he gets off scot-free. He gets to be a big sports star, and what do you get? A bad reputation." He looked toward the kitchen. "Your mother and I have been talking about moving."

The words took Chevon's breath away. *No.* "Wait."

He looked at her, surprised, as if she'd been audacious to even speak. He waited expectantly, but now she was scared to say anything. So she said nothing.

"I apologize for losing my cool. But you've got to understand that I have a reason to be angry. And I forbid you from seeing that boy. I expect you to abide by that, or we're going to have a serious problem."

Suddenly, Chevon desperately wanted to be with Jason. "I have to get to school."

"I understand you have a crush on the boy—"

How incredibly patronizing. She wasn't ten years old. She didn't have *crushes*.

—"but I assure you. He's not worth it."

Her mom came into the room with toast held out, but Chevon didn't take it. She had no interest in food.

"So you're not going to school. Your mother will go in and pick up your books and assignments. And she has made an appointment for you for Monday morning. Until then, you're staying right here."

Chevon's mouth dropped open. "That's ridiculous!"

"We wouldn't have to do it if you had gotten out of his car last night. But it's obvious that you can't be trusted. Your mother has been going on and on about how levelheaded you are, but I had my doubts. Levelheaded girls don't get pregnant at sixteen. And now you've proven that there is nothing level about your head. So give me your phone."

"What?" she cried. Where was this coming from? "Why?"

"Because I don't even want you talking to him!" He held his hand out. "Now, where is it?" There was no way she was giving him her phone. Not in a billion years. She stood up and headed for the door, frantic to get out of there.

"Phil, you said you would be calm."

"I'm trying." He beat Chevon to the door and put his hand on it. "You can relax and eat your breakfast and enjoy some television, or you can go to your room. Either way give me your phone."

"Dad!" she screamed. "I have to go to school! I have a game today!" She didn't care anything about that game. She didn't even know if she'd be allowed to play, but she knew her dad cared about basketball.

"A game?" he bellowed. "How stupid do you think we are? Do you really think your coach hasn't called and checked on you? She said you walked out of her gym!" He got right in her face and swore. "What is wrong with you? Who are you? What happened to my daughter?"

For the first time ever, she was scared of her father. She didn't think he would hit her, but she didn't know what he *would* do. He started grabbing for her pockets trying to find the phone.

"Phil! Stop!"

Her mom grabbed for his arm, and Chevon ran for the stairs, catching her toe on the second one and sprawling as she tried to scramble up them. When she got to the top, she turned and hollered down at them, "By the way, you can't make me get an abortion. I looked it up online. I am having this baby." She had wanted to make her father angry, and it worked.

He opened his mouth and just bellowed. No words came out, just a roar of rage.

"Are you insane?" her mother asked. "How are you going to raise a baby? You're not doing it in this house! Your appointment is Monday morning! Now go to your—"

"I have lots of help. Jason will help. Jason's father will help. Jason's church will help."

Her mother laughed snidely. "Oh yeah, I'm sure his church will be excited about helping a pregnant teen."

The laugh infuriated her more than the words. "They will!" she screamed. "They've already promised!"

Her mom put her hands on her hips and looked up at her. "Who has promised?"

Chevon turned to go to her room.

"Chevon, wait!"

Chevon hesitated.

"Who has promised?" her mother repeated.

She turned slowly to face her mother, surprised her father wasn't on his way up the stairs. She guessed he didn't need to be. He had her trapped now, and that's all he wanted. "I have friends at that church, and they promised to help. They said they would help for the baby's entire life."

Her mother laughed again. "You are so naïve. They're trying to turn you into some pro-life poster child, but they will abandon you the second you have that baby. The second it's too late to do the right thing, they'll forget you even exist. What kind of help are you expecting from them, exactly? Are they going to help you when the baby's crying all night, night after night? Are they going to help when you can't work, can't afford daycare, and can't pay the bills? Are they going to help when you realize you've ruined your life?

What are they going to do for you then?" Her mother sounded as if she knew what she was talking about.

"It doesn't matter," she spat out. "I still have Jason and his father."

"You don't *have* Jason," her mother said as her father hollered, "I forbid you from ever seeing that boy again! Now get into your room before I put you there!"

She ran to her room and slammed the door behind her. Instinctively she ran into the corner of her room and then turned and looked at the door. Her whole body shook. She pulled out her phone and texted, "Scared. Parents flipping. Can you come get me?"

She stared at the phone desperately willing him to answer, but he didn't. She heard her father on the stairs and rushed to lock the door. She looked at her window. She didn't think she could climb out it, but she was almost willing to try.

She heard her father lean against the door and stepped away from it.

"Sweetie, I'm sorry. I don't know how to handle this. I need to protect you. You can come out if you want to, but I want you to stay home for now. You need to trust me. I'm doing what's best for you." How he managed to suddenly be calm after being so wild, Chevon didn't know. But then, she'd never seen him that wild.

She went to her window and looked outside. Then she looked down at her phone. Why wasn't Jason answering? She looked out the window again. She had to get out of this house. There was a tree about six feet away. Could she reach it? Or maybe it was ten feet. She didn't know, and she started to cry harder, whimpering at her own stupidity. She was so disgusted with herself.

Suddenly, a surge of confidence coursed through her. Stop being such a wuss, she told herself and flung the window open. She might break both legs, but she'd rather do that than stay in this house. She stuck her head out into the cold and then swung one leg over the windowsill. She reached out for the tree, but it might as well have been a million miles away. She looked around for other options, but there weren't any. She looked down. How far was that drop?

It looked doable. She swung her other leg out and then slowly lowered herself, keeping her elbows on the windowsill. Then, when most of her body was dangling, she tried to transfer her weight to her hands instead of her elbows—and failed. Her fingers slipped and she grabbed and clawed for purchase, trying to slow her descent, but it was too late.

She looked down, and what she saw gave her hope. She might survive this. She bent her knees, and when her toes hit the ground, she forced herself into a somersault. Then she lay there on the ground surprised at how okay she felt. She sat up and checked herself over, but everything appeared to be in working order. Relief rushed through her, and she climbed to her feet and brushed the wet leaves off her pants. She headed into the woods, and as soon as her house was out of sight, she turned and walked toward the road. She texted Jason. "I snuck out. Can you come pick me up? Walking toward school."

She reached the road and looked down at her phone. Why wasn't he texting back? She shivered. It was cold out. And she wasn't wearing a coat. She touched her stomach. If she got too cold, would it hurt the baby? This new fear was overwhelming. If she hurt this baby because she'd been stubborn and sneaked out of her house, that would be so stupid. She wouldn't deserve to have a baby—ever. She started walking faster. She looked at her phone again. Where was Jason?

She could text Hype, but she was too embarrassed. What about Zoe? She didn't have her number. She looked her up on social media, sent her a contact request, and then sent her a message. She told her where she was and asked her to find Jason. She pressed send and then kept typing. "I'm scared I might be too cold. Please hurry."

She pressed send again.

Chapter 32

Zoe

Zoe was beyond shocked to receive a message from Chevon. She answered immediately. "On it." Except that Jason wasn't in the classroom. She looked around in case she'd missed him, though the chances of that were slim.

Where could he have gone? He had picked her up and driven her to school like always. So why was he so late to class?

She got excused to go to the bathroom and then wandered around the school looking for him. She checked the library, which was silly. He never went to the library. She checked the gym and the weight room. She didn't dare check the boys' locker room or the boys' bathroom. As she stood outside the latter, staring at the door, wondering how to proceed, Levi came out. He stopped quickly when he saw her.

Without thinking, she asked, "Is Jason in there?"

He grimaced. "You're kidding."

"No, it's not like that," she said quickly. "Chevon is ..." She stopped, unsure if Chevon's predicament was supposed to be a secret.

"Chevon is what?"

"She's in trouble, and she asked me to find Jason so he can go get her out of it."

Levi lowered his voice. "What kind of trouble?"

She hesitated again.

"Spit it out."

Fine. "She's trying to walk to school, and she's really cold."

He looked disappointed.

He had a point. That didn't sound like an exceptionally dangerous predicament when she said it aloud. "Well ... I don't think she should get too cold because of the ... you know."

Understanding registered on his face. "Oh right." He looked up and down the hallway. "Come on, I'll take you." He took off.

After a brief hesitation, she followed. "Do you have your mom's car again?"

He looked back over his shoulder without slowing down. "Are you making fun of me?"

"Of course not," she said quickly. "My mom won't even let me touch her car." She had to hurry to keep up with his long legs. "Are we just going to go out the front door?" She didn't think that was a good idea.

"Of course not. Do you think this is my first rodeo?"

She followed him into the cafeteria.

"We'll go out the back."

"And then what?" She didn't understand how they were going to drive anywhere without a car.

"Then we'll take Kendall's car."

Kendall had bothered to come to school that day? "Are you still friends with him?"

"Definitely not. But I can still take his car." Then more quietly, Levi added, "And then once we get Chevon dropped off at school, we can drive it off a cliff."

They scurried through the dark gym and then out the back door, and sure enough, there was Kendall's car sitting there looking all innocent.

Were they really going to steal a car? Zoe only hesitated for a few seconds. Then she figured that Levi would be the one on the hook for it if they got caught.

Kendall's keys were above the visor. Levi didn't even look anywhere else first.

Zoe shut the door. "Kendall's fairly predictable, huh?"

"Usually." He started the car and backed out.

"You're not the least bit nervous about getting in trouble?"

He shrugged. "Maybe now that you mention it. I usually don't think about that stuff."

She smiled. She found this endearing.

Levi looked at the gas gauge and swore. "Figures."

Zoe reached into her pocket and felt her lunch money. "I have a few dollars."

"No, let's get as far as we can go. If we run out of gas, I'll call my mom. I'd rather walk around the peninsula than squirt any money into his tank."

Zoe smiled again, caught herself, and forced herself to stop smiling. She wasn't supposed to be having this much fun. "Do you know where she lives?"

"Of course. It's a small peninsula."

"Have you lived here your whole life?"

He gave her a long look, and she grew nervous that he wasn't watching the road. Finally, he answered her. "Sure have."

They met a police car, and Zoe stiffened.

"Relax. If we get stopped, I'll say I kidnapped you."

She giggled. "That probably wouldn't help matters much." She tried to think of something else to say, but her mind was blank. In her hurry to go rescue Chevon, she hadn't thought about the fact that she was getting into a car to be alone with Levi. Now that she was here, she felt a little awkward. "Want some music?"

"Sure."

Relieved, she reached for the knob.

One and a half bad songs later, they saw Chevon walking down the road in a T-shirt.

"Oh yeah," Levi said. "She *is* cold." He gave it more gas.

Chevon hesitated but then hurried toward the car and ripped the back door open. "Thank you," she said, sounding completely unlike herself.

Levi reached down and cranked up the heat. "Slide toward the middle. It'll be warmer there."

Chevon did as she was told, and Levi turned the car around.

"You okay?" Zoe turned to look at her.

"Yeah. Scared me to death when I thought you'd brought Kendall. I thought I'd have to choose between him and freezing to death." She looked at Levi. "Thanks, Levi."

"No prob. My plan is to park this car right where we found it. So don't mention to Kendall that he helped rescue you."

She snickered. "I am so cold."

"Been there. You'll feel better soon."

Wow. Zoe sneaked a look at Levi. He sounded as if he really cared. Were he and Chevon close? She didn't think so. She'd never seen them anywhere near each other.

Levi's plan worked. They parked the car, he placed the keys back above the visor, and then Chevon thanked him again.

Zoe echoed her, "Yeah, thanks, Levi."

Levi gave her a small smile, which was somehow a little sad. "You're welcome."

Chevon pulled on the school's back door. It didn't open. "How are we going to get in?" She obviously hadn't tried sneaking into school an hour late before.

"Hang on. I'll run around to the front and then come let you in."

"But you're going to get caught," Zoe said.

"No, I won't. I'm not going in through the front door. I'll knock on the shop window. They'll let me climb in."

Zoe laughed. "Are you serious?"

He ripped his flannel shirt off and handed it to Chevon. "I'll hurry. Jump up and down till I get back." Then, with surprising speed, he sprinted toward the front of the building.

Zoe watched Chevon put on Levi's shirt and was stunned to realize that she was a little jealous.

Chapter 33

Chevon

"Why haven't you answered your phone?" Chevon scolded and then looked around self-consciously. She hadn't meant to sound so dramatic.

Jason looked guilty. "Sorry. I was with the counselor."

"The counselor? Why, what's wrong?" She felt stupid. "I mean, apart from the obvious."

"Nothing's wrong. Somebody called the office and said that I needed counseling." He gave her a hard look. "I'm assuming it was your parents."

What? Why would they do that? "I don't think so."

"Really? Because the guidance counselor worked pretty hard to get me to consider my options." His fingers made air quotes around the word *options*.

"What? She tried to talk you into abortion?"

Jason's confidence flickered. It was a nice change of pace. "Not exactly. I don't know. It seemed like that's what she was doing, but maybe I'm paranoid. Either way, she wanted to make sure I knew that was an option."

As far as Chevon was concerned, it still was.

Maybe.

"Why, what did you need?"

"Oh my word, my parents have lost their minds."

He didn't believe her. Or he believed her, but he didn't understand. Either way, he wasn't nearly concerned enough.

"I'm serious. Like really lost it. Like my father wouldn't let me out of the house. I had to jump out my window and walk to school and I almost froze to death, and I had to call Zoe, and she had to get Levi to come get me and—"

"Levi came to get you? How?"

That was the part that alarmed him? Not that she'd thrown her pregnant butt out a second-story window. She rolled her eyes. *Boys.* "Never mind Levi. The point is that my father is on a warpath. He's not going to let me have any say in this." Her voice broke, and tears threatened.

Jason reached out for her arm, but then dropped his hand. What a wuss.

"I'm sorry," he said lamely.

"So I'm here now, but I can't exactly go home." She waited for him to say something, for him to tell her where to go, for him to invite her to go with him, for him to promise to take care of her.

Of course, he did none of that. Why had she expected anything different? He was a dumb jock. An arrogant, selfish, dumb jock.

The bell rang, but neither of them moved.

"I don't know what to do, Jason."

"I'm sorry," he said again.

She was tired of hearing that. She wanted him to tell her what to do. Not that she'd listen, but at least she'd have another voice to listen to, other than the dozen voices of her own arguing inside her head. She stepped closer. "Maybe we should just do it."

"Do what?"

"You know, get it done. Then everything could go back to normal." Part of her cried out against this option. Part of her found tremendous comfort in it.

"Chevon." He reached up and touched her cheek with the back of his hand, and this touch was more encouraging than any words from him could have been. "No matter what you decide, I don't think anything is ever going to go back to normal. We've changed. The whole world has changed."

She started. "Wow, Jason DeGrave. I think that's the wisest thing I've ever heard you say." Maybe the only wise thing she'd ever heard him say. She smirked.

"Thanks. I think." He tipped his head sideways. "Since you never compliment me, now when you do, I'm not sure if you're messing with me."

She laughed, and half of her panic left her. "I wasn't this time. Promise."

"Get to class!" The assistant principal stood at the end of the hall, his arms crossed in front of him, glaring at them.

"Come on." She turned away from the hall monitor and started walking.

"Class is the other direction."

Obviously. "I know that. Pregnancy doesn't make me stupid." She rounded the corner and stopped. "I wanted to ask you something else."

"What?" He looked hopeful as if she were going to ask him something wonderful.

She almost rolled her eyes again. What a weirdo he was. "My mom said that your church friends are full of ... well, she said they were *full*. She said they won't actually help me, that they're just saying that so I will have the baby."

He frowned. "Why would they do that?"

"I don't know. I don't know if it makes sense. She said they're trying to use me for some pro-life political thing."

Jason was still confused. "I don't know what your mom's talking about, but I do know that they will help you. Rachel doesn't lie. Neither does Esther. And even if they don't help you, which they will, but even if the church burns down and we can't find any Christians, I will still help you. I will never abandon you."

Warmth flooded through her, and she nearly wept right there in the hallway. She wanted to topple forward and bury her head in his chest and thank him. Of course, she didn't. "Thank you," she said, managing to make her gratitude sound completely void of emotion. "Should we go to class now?"

He looked back the way they'd come. "Uh ... we have to go back past Mr. Cords."

"That's all right. I'll tell him pregnancy makes me stupid."

Jason looked unsure if he was allowed to laugh.

She elbowed him playfully. "Come on. Let's go get educated. We're going to need it."

Chapter 34

Esther

As Zoe ran through her warm-up routine, Esther beamed with pride and didn't try to hide it. Though Zoe had made it clear through her constant self-deprecation that she didn't think she was improving, Esther now knew that wasn't true.

Instead of looking terrified, Zoe now looked focused. Incredibly focused. Esther couldn't believe how seriously she was taking this, especially with everything that was going on with her friends. Maybe basketball was giving her a healthy distraction. For the millionth time that day, Esther silently prayed for Chevon. Then she scanned the gym for the young woman but didn't see her. Instead, her eyes landed on a couple sitting behind the team's bench. Both of them stared at her. She locked eyes with them and realized their attention was not friendly. She broke the contact as she mumbled to Walter, "Why are those people behind the bench glaring at me?"

Walter furrowed his brow. "Those are the Shermans."

"Chevon's parents?" She squinted, trying to see if that was the woman who had once sold her Tupperware. She couldn't tell.

"Yes. My guess would be that they have associated you with New Beginnings and that they are not happy that the church is interfering with their daughter's life." Walter's normally diplomatic tone had a critical edge to it.

Esther looked at him, surprised. "Do you think we are overstepping?"

He hesitated. "Will you be mad at me if I say yes?"

"Of course not." She wished she hadn't asked. She wanted to go back to admiring Zoe's dribbling. "We don't have to agree on everything."

He took a deep breath. "I'm not saying you're wrong. But I think we should tread carefully. She's a child, and we don't really know what we're doing."

"Of course we know what we're doing!" she cried, indignant.

He gave her a sardonic look.

Oh yeah. She had encouraged disagreement, and then as soon as he'd disagreed with her, she'd argued. "Sorry," she said softly.

"We are not medical professionals. We are not counselors. We're trying to help her make a decision that will have consequences we can't possibly understand."

She vehemently disagreed, but she forced herself to process his words, to try to understand his point of view. "You can look at this situation as incredibly complex with a million different factors. Or you can look at it with only two factors, life or death."

He subtly shook his head. "I don't think it can be that simple."

She didn't want to argue with him anymore, so she turned her attention back to Zoe just in time for the buzzer to sound. She watched her granddaughter trot toward the bench and realized Chevon's parents were still glaring across the gym. Why were they here when Chevon wasn't?

Though Zoe started the game sitting on the bench, she still looked incredibly focused. She sat with her elbow on her knee, her head on her hand, chewing her nails as her eyes followed the ball up and down the court.

As Esther watched her granddaughter watch the game and tried to avoid the frequent glances from Chevon's parents, she heard a chilling cry of pain. The whistle blew, and she looked to see Callie writhing on the floor.

The mother in her went on high alert, and she reached for Walter's hand. "Oh no!"

The ref motioned toward the coach, and she and someone carrying a tiny medical bag hurried out onto the court, but Callie was already getting up. She wiped her tears off on the shoulder of her uniform and then started hobbling toward the bench. The coach grabbed her and helped her as the fans clapped her off the floor.

Coach Hodges pointed to Zoe and then pointed toward the score table.

Now Zoe's face registered panic, but she got up, ripped off her warm-up shirt, and ran over to kneel in front of the score table. The ref waved her on as Coach hollered at another girl to take over point guard and give Zoe the spot under the hoop.

The game restarted, and they gave Zoe the ball. She caught it above her head, turned, and shot without bringing the ball down. It went through the hoop, and though Esther's heart nearly leapt out of her chest, she clapped politely. Walter showed no such restraint. He leapt to his feet, clapped, cheered, and stomped his foot, shaking the bleachers. Not far away, Levi cheered with a similar enthusiasm. Esther smiled. She was growing quite fond of Levi.

On the next trip down the court, the girls did nearly the same play. Zoe caught the ball, spun, and shot from the same spot, about two feet away from the basket. She missed this time, but she caught the rebound and shot again. Again she missed, again she got her own rebound, and again she shot. The ball went in, and the gym erupted with applause.

Her determination was surprising. Her focus was surprising. The fact that the ball went in was surprising. But what was most surprising was the small smile she wore on her face as she ran back down the court to play defense.

Esther shook her head. Zoe was blossoming into a whole new woman, right before her eyes.

When the halftime buzzer sounded, Zoe had eight points and grinned all the way to the locker room.

"This is amazing," Walter said. "Good for her."

Esther continued to watch her walk away, but Walter's eyes drifted across the gym, and she felt him stiffen. As her eyes followed his, he wrapped his arm around her protectively. Chevon's parents were headed their way.

"You're Zoe's grandmother," the man said.

Esther wasn't sure if it was a question. Walter stood and went down to the floor to stand beside them. He offered his hand. "Nice to see you, Phil. Yes, this is Esther, Zoe's grandmother."

Though the man looked flummoxed, he accepted the handshake. "We're Chevon's parents."

Walter didn't say anything, and Esther found his lack of response painfully awkward. She forced a smile, though these people were making her uncomfortable. "We are very fond of Chevon," she said to fill the space.

Phil nearly snarled. "You don't need to be. Chevon does not need your fondness. Now where is she?"

Esther reared back.

"Where is who?" Walter asked, though the answer was obvious.

"My daughter," Phil said, his words dripping with hatred.

Again Walter didn't say anything, and again Esther felt pressured to speak, but she was starting to think Walter had the right idea with his silence, so she bit her lip.

"They don't know where she is," Mary said softly.

"We called all her friends," Phil said. "We hoped she'd be here supporting her team, but ..." Anger overtook him, and he couldn't finish his sentence.

It almost seemed he was accusing them of convincing Chevon to betray her team.

"We certainly don't know where she is," Walter said evenly, "but we will let you know if we see her or hear from her. Could I have a phone number?" He pulled out his phone.

Mary stepped closer again and recited the phone number while Phil continued to glare at Esther. She wanted them to go away. She couldn't remember the last time anyone had shown her this much hostility.

Walter tucked his phone back into his pocket and asked, "Have you tracked her phone?"

Esther looked at him quickly. It was a sound idea, of course, but she wasn't sure they should help this angry man find his daughter. Chevon was probably tucked away somewhere safe, purposely avoiding said anger.

Phil stared at Walter. "Track her phone?"

Esther scanned the gym, looking for Jason, but then realized he wouldn't be there. They were playing away that night. Probably a good thing for Jason not to be in the same gym as this man, but that also meant that wherever Chevon was, she wasn't tucked away safely with Jason.

"Sure. Most cell carriers offer that option in case you lose your phone."

Phil looked at his wife. "Let's go." He headed for the gym door, and Mary, with her head down, followed her husband.

Esther exhaled. "Phew. That was awful."

Walter returned to his seat beside her. "Yes, it was. And I'm sorry he's focusing on you to blame, but ..."

"But what?"

"But if I were in his shoes, I'd probably be just as angry, and I'm not sure I'd know who to blame either."

Chapter 35

Rachel

Rachel held the hot mug out to Chevon. "Sorry that it's cracked, but that's the biggest one I have. I figured you'd rather have a heaping portion than an uncracked cup."

Chevon took the cup from her outstretched hand with a smile so genuine Rachel's heart surged with love. "I'm just so happy to have chocolate."

"I can appreciate that." Rachel settled into her armchair and eyed Chevon. She was thrilled the girl was there and wanted her to feel comfortable, but she had to make sure that her parents knew where she was, and she didn't know how to do that without Chevon thinking she was siding with them. The brief version of the story that Chevon had shared suggested that her father was behaving something like a monster right now. Rachel wasn't sure this was an accurate portrayal, but she didn't want Chevon to think she was siding with a monster over her.

Instead of talking, Rachel took a sip from her own mug, which was also cracked.

"So, how much does this childbirth hurt anyway?" Chevon laughed, but her eyes were sober.

"It hurts a lot."

Chevon snickered. "That's not what I expected you to say."

"Would you like me to lie to you?"

"Maybe?" She giggled again but her eyes remained serious.

"Every pregnancy is different. Even two deliveries for the same woman can be vastly different. My daughter wasn't so bad, so I went into my second delivery a bit cocky, and my son didn't want to come out. That was a long labor, and it hurt so bad I was afraid something was really wrong. But now looking back I think my fear made the pain worse." She shrugged. "It will be hard, but probably not as hard as you're thinking. Your body knows how to do it. God has already programmed it to do its job. So don't worry about that. You can't mess it up. Just make sure you have one or two people in there with you who love you and will encourage you. That will help. And know that even long labors are over quickly. It's just a blip on the timeline of your child's life." She took a sip of her cocoa. "You should talk to my friend Cathy about it. She's better at explaining things and describing things than I am."

"I think you do a great job. Better than Google did anyway."

Rachel chuckled. "I wouldn't trust an internet search with anything. Have you asked your mom that question?"

Chevon shook her head. "I wanted to, but there hasn't been the right time ... and I didn't want her to think that I was considering having the baby."

Rachel was tempted to respond to this but didn't.

"I still can't believe I'm referring to it as a baby. If I'm going to end this pregnancy, I need to stop thinking like that. It's not a baby yet."

Rachel couldn't resist. "I think we both know that it is."

Chevon looked up quickly.

"I will support you and love you no matter what you do, but we both know it's a baby already. It's a tiny person, and you're the only person it knows."

Chevon gasped. "That's a lot of pressure!"

"Sorry. But the pressure you're feeling is not from me. Your life has taken a pretty drastic turn, and it's your life that's putting the pressure on you. Life does that to us all the time, often when we're least expecting it. But in between those moments of intense pressure, there are long peaceful seasons of joy. Even during labor, you'll be screaming one second and feeling great the next. Then you'll scream again." She laughed. "Then you'll feel great. And then you'll have a baby in your arms. A perfect little piece of paradise."

"Wow. You sure are trying to talk me into having a baby, aren't you?"

That's why you came here to hide out, Rachel thought, because you wanted to be talked into having a baby. "I do what I can."

"I appreciate your honesty."

"That's refreshing. Often people don't." It was now or never. "Speaking of honesty, I really think you should text your parents and tell them that you're safe. You don't have to tell them where you are, but it's making me ill to think how worried they must be right now."

"Yeah right," Chevon scoffed. "My dad is probably glad I'm gone and hoping I don't come back." She looked thoughtful, and Rachel forced herself to give her time to think. Sure enough, Chevon pulled her phone out of her back pocket. "I'll text my mom, though. You're right. She probably is worried, and I don't want her to be." She texted something quickly and then tucked her phone back away and looked at Rachel. "Why am I having so much trouble deciding? One second, I think, yes, I'm definitely doing this. I'm going to marry Jason DeGrave and have his babies and live in this town for the rest of my life and that will be fine. The next second I'm terrified and I hate Jason and I want to run away and never come back to this town again."

Rachel laughed. "That sounds about right."

Chevon's phone dinged, and she hesitated but then pulled it out of her pocket. She read the message, didn't share it with Rachel, and put the phone away again.

Rachel silently prayed for Chevon's mother.

Chevon looked at Rachel. "My mom says that you guys won't really help me, that you just want me to do what you think is right, and then you'll forget all about me."

Rachel shook her head quickly, anger rising in her chest. "That's because your mother doesn't know what it means to be a follower of Jesus."

Chevon scowled.

"When you experience the love of Jesus personally, when you experience what he can do in your life, you love other people in a way that is hard to imagine if you haven't been through it. I genuinely love you. I want to spend time with you, and I will want to spend time with your baby. And I will want you and your little family to be happy and successful, and I will work to make that happen. And my sisters in Christ feel the same way."

Someone pounded on Rachel's door, and the color drained from Chevon's face.

"If that's your parents," Rachel said quickly, getting up, "don't panic." She stepped closer to the girl. "They can't make you do anything you don't want to do. They are still your parents, they still love you, and they still want what's best for you even if they don't know what that is." She forced eye contact with the trembling girl. "Breathe. You can do this." The pounding came again, and Rachel glanced toward the door. "Besides, it might not even be your parents."

Except that it was. The man pushed past her and charged into her house. Fearing he was going to hurt Chevon, she hurried to pass him and planted herself between him and his daughter. But he stopped several feet short of Chevon and pointed at the door. "Get in the car!" he shouted, using several expletives to emphasize the urgency of his request.

"No!" Chevon screamed. "I am perfectly safe here!"

"Do not make me sling you over my shoulder because I will!" He stepped toward her.

"Wait!" Rachel shouted with an authority that surprised her.

The man didn't stop but he slowed down as he looked at her.

"I will help you!" she said quickly.

He stopped moving.

"I'm on your side," she continued. "Can you just give me two minutes alone with Chevon's mother? Then she and Chevon will walk out of this house calmly."

Chevon's dad looked at his wife as if he didn't quite trust her, and she gave him a mousy nod. Slowly, he backed toward the door.

"Thank you."

He gave Rachel a poisoned look but kept moving. "I've had about enough of you church ladies and your meddling." He looked at his wife and held up two fingers. "Two minutes and then I'm coming back in and then we're *leaving*."

She gave no response.

As soon as he was out, Rachel hurried to shut the door behind him. "What's your name?" she asked quickly.

"Mary."

"Mary, I'm Rachel." She stopped and stood in front of the woman. "And I really am on your side. I have a very serious question, and you need to tell me the truth. Does that man ever hit you or your daughter?"

Mary shook her head rapidly. "Absolutely not. He's been a model father and husband until all this started."

Chevon also nodded. "He won't hurt me, Rachel. I'm scared of him right now, but he won't physically hurt me."

Relief washed over Rachel. "That's so good to hear." She put her hands on Chevon's shoulders and kissed her on the forehead. "Go with your parents, honey. I'm still here for you, but go with your parents. Ask God to help you. Ask him to help you make the right decision and ask him to help your parents understand that decision, whatever it is."

Her eyes filled with tears. "I don't want to go with them."

"I know, but they are your parents. This is their job, so let them do it. And I promise you, if you let God help you, this is all going to work out, and you're going to look back on this and think, 'Wow, look at what God did!'" She took one hand off Chevon's shoulder and spun to look at her mother. "I'll be praying for both of you. Now go. Before our two minutes are up."

Chapter 36

Zoe

"Double digits!" Walter cried when he saw Zoe coming. He held his hand up for a high five, which she awkwardly granted. What was he talking about?

"You had twelve points! That's double digits, which is a big deal."

Something swelled in her chest. Was that pride? She tried to hide it. "Oh, I didn't know that was a thing."

Walter laughed. "It's definitely a thing. Most ballplayers have to work really hard to get double digits, but you seem to be a natural."

Zoe didn't feel like a natural at anything except maybe getting into trouble. She saw Levi walking toward her, and her stomach did a somersault.

He flashed his lazy smile. "Great game, hot stuff."

She blinked. Hot stuff? This was absurd, and yet she loved it.

"I have my mom's car." He winked. "Would you like a ride home?"

Her mouth fell open to decline his offer, but no sound came out. To avoid looking at Levi, she looked at her grandmother, who looked just as scared as she felt.

"Oh, go ahead, Zoe," Walter said. "Your grandmother can live without you for a few minutes."

Did Walter really think she'd hesitated because she was worried about her grandmother's loneliness? She doubted it. So Walter was trying to rescue her from her social awkwardness? Probably. This made her like Walter a lot. But did she even want to ride home with Levi? It seemed it was about to happen whether she wanted it or not. She forced herself to look at Levi and tried to smile.

Doubt flickered across his face, but he didn't verbalize it. He looked at Esther. "I'll have her home in a jiffy." He turned back to Zoe and held a hand out. "You want some help with your bag?"

Without thinking, she quickly said, "No."

He looked disappointed, but that was ridiculous. It was a ten-pound backpack. Why would she need help carrying it to the car? She'd been carrying backpacks to cars since kindergarten, and no one had ever offered to help her. He meandered toward the door, and she fell into step beside him. "Kinda surprised to see you at the games. Didn't think sports were your thing."

"Why would you think that?"

She remembered Jason distinctly saying that sports weren't Levi's thing, but she knew better than to quote Jason. "I don't know."

"You're right. They're definitely not my thing, but I've been trying to find more wholesome forms of entertainment." He snickered. "Besides, I like watching you play." He opened the door for her and looked at her, and she realized she was looking up into his eyes. This came as a shock.

"What?" he asked as they stepped out into the cold darkness.

"Nothing."

"It wasn't nothing. You look surprised at something."

"Did you grow?"

He laughed. "Not lately, thank goodness. I think I'm gangly enough."

She didn't say anything, and he opened the car door for her. Before getting in she stopped and looked at him. Yup, sure enough, she was looking up into his eyes. She leaned over the door and looked at his boots. "Are you wearing lifts?" She meant it as a joke, but he didn't laugh.

"Of course not. What's the matter with you?"

Now she was embarrassed. She shrugged and stepped back. "I don't know. I just didn't think you were taller than me."

"Well, you really shouldn't judge a guy based on how tall he is when he's half-dead in a haunted basement."

She laughed. This was an excellent point. "Fair enough. Sorry."

"No harm done." He shut the door behind her.

He started the car. "So that's a big deal to you? You monitor a lot of people's heights?"

"No," she said defensively. "That would be pretty weird. I'm just used to being the tallest, so when someone is taller than me, I notice."

"Well, your tallness certainly played in your favor tonight. You were amazing."

That prideful swelling returned, and this time she let it happen. She was in a dark car. No one could see her beaming.

"I was proud to be your friend tonight." He put the car in drive and looked at her. "I am your friend, right?"

"Of course," Zoe said quickly. "Why wouldn't you be?"

"Well ... I sort of told you I liked you, and then you sort of freaked out. So I just wanted to tell you that I do want to be your friend." He took his hands off the wheel and held them up. "No strings attached."

These words should have brought her relief, but they didn't.

"So, how goes the drama with Chevon and Jason?"

Zoe groaned. She'd gone a few hours without thinking about them, and hadn't it been grand.

Chapter 37

Zoe

"Dude! Where's Chevon?"

Jason's eyes widened. "Why, was I supposed to pick her up?"

Zoe threw her bag into the back. "Not that I know of, but Gramma said there was some drama at the game last night."

"What are you talking about?" He was frustrated. Jason was never outside of the know.

"I don't really understand it. Chevon's parents were at the game, and they came and hollered at Gramma and asked her why she was hiding Chevon or something like that."

"No way." He sounded worried.

"What? Do you think something is actually wrong? I figured she was hiding from them somewhere."

"Yeah, that's probably it, but she's not texting me either. I haven't heard from her since last night."

"Last night? *Whoa*. Let's all panic. Maybe she was, I don't know, sleeping?"

He gave her side-eye. "You are so funny. I'm serious. Lately we've been texting each other right before we go to bed."

Zoe braced herself, expecting this information to cause that familiar sickness of jealousy, but it didn't happen.

"So I texted her right before bed, and she didn't answer. No big deal. But I texted her this morning, and still no answer. I wasn't worried until you just told me that she's missing."

Zoe felt bad for causing him more stress. "I'm sure she's not *missing*. Let's not be dramatic. Like I said, she's just hiding from her parents."

"That doesn't explain why she'd be hiding from me."

Zoe didn't think this was that much of a stretch. If she were in Chevon's shoes, she would be hiding from *everybody*. "I'm sure she'll be at school, and she can explain herself to you. But go easy."

"Of course I'd go easy. I would never be hard on Chevon."

Zoe heard a fondness in his voice, and again, her heart didn't react the way she'd expected it to. If anything, she was relieved to hear him speaking fondly of Chevon instead of Alita.

"I know you wouldn't. Sorry. I just feel bad for her. And I feel bad for you too. I know this isn't easy on anybody. So I didn't mean to scare you. Sorry. I'm sure she'll be in first period. She's probably already there."

Except that she wasn't.

And she wasn't in second period either. Zoe walked into the classroom right behind Jason, who put his books down, looked around the room, and then picked his books up again. "I'm going to go look for her."

"She's still not answering your texts?"

He shook his head, and he looked pale. "No, and that's super weird. I think something's wrong."

This time, Zoe believed him. "You want me to go with you?" As soon as she said the words, she regretted them. Why would he want her to go with him to check on his new girlfriend? But she'd only meant to be helpful. And maybe to get out of school. "Sorry, that's stupid."

He leveled a gaze at her. "No, it's not stupid. Would you?"

She nodded.

"Okay, I'll leave. Wait a few seconds and then follow me." And then he was gone.

The teacher, a curious look on his face, watched Jason's back until it disappeared and then looked at Zoe as if she were going to explain Jason's departure. She quickly looked down at her notebook and waited for the teacher to become preoccupied with something else, and then she scurried out of the room as well.

She stopped at her locker to get her coat, and the hallways were empty. Where had Jason gone? Was he already outside? She tried to act naturally, which wasn't easy in the empty hallway when she felt like a million eyes were watching her even though she couldn't see any, but when she reached the cafeteria, she started speed-walking. Suddenly, she was sure Jason had left her.

She flew out the back door to find him idling just outside it, as if she were the bank robber and he the getaway driver. She jumped into the front seat. "Drive!" she cried, and he looked bewildered.

"Just trying to be funny," she said sheepishly. "Drive," she repeated in a more appropriate tone.

He shook his head and drove away.

She watched the school fade in her side mirror. She hadn't gotten caught the last time she'd ditched school. But if she ever did get caught for one of these stunts, she was probably going to get suspended.

She looked over at her chauffeur. Or maybe not, if she was with Jason.

Suddenly, she missed Levi. She wished they'd invited him to come along.

Chapter 38

Jason

Jason glanced over at his partner. He was really grateful for Zoe's friendship. All his guy friends had started acting like he was contagious—even Hype. He wondered if he'd have any friends left once he became a father. Yes, he'd still have Zoe.

But how weird was it that he was bringing her along on this mission? Should a grown man really bring a female friend along when trying to rescue the woman he loved? The thought nearly knocked the wind out of him. Loved? Where had that come from? He shook his head. Come on, Jason, back to earth. The truth was that he had invited Zoe because he was scared of Chevon's father. He didn't know what he expected Zoe to do, but her presence made him a little less scared. Again, a grown man shouldn't be scared of a girl's father.

But he was. And he always felt ashamed when he was around the man, like he had violated his daughter or something. He certainly hadn't meant to do that. He hadn't wanted anything but to be close to Chevon. And over the last few horrible weeks, that desire had intensified to a strength he almost couldn't stand.

"Are we going to her house?" Zoe sounded nervous.

Maybe his fear was rubbing off on her. "That's my plan."

"But she's not there."

"Why do you think that?"

"Because they couldn't find her last night."

"I think they did find her. That's the only explanation I can come up with for why she's not answering me. I think they took her phone away. Because if they didn't, the only other theories I can come up with are really scary. You know all those bad things we were worried had happened to Levi? Well, now I'm thinking all those same thoughts about Chevon."

"Chevon isn't stupid, though. She doesn't do stupid things and get herself into stupid situations." Though she was being incredibly critical of Levi, there was a weird fondness in her voice.

He looked at her curiously. "That's true. Thank you."

They pulled into Chevon's driveway, and he took his foot off the gas. The car slowed to a crawl and then almost stopped.

"You don't have to do this."

He stepped on the gas. "Yes, I do."

He stopped the car in front of her steps and looked up at the front door. Get a grip, he told himself. Be a man.

"Do you want me to go to the door for you? Might be less confrontational—"

"No," he said quickly. "Thank you for being here, but please let me do this part by myself. I'm trying to save what little pride I have left." He got out of the car and forced himself to breathe. It was true that he was trying to redeem some scrap of self-respect, but he also wanted to impress Chevon. He was scared of her father, but he couldn't let that show. He had to show her that he was just as much a man as her father was. Worried he might throw up on their front steps, he knocked on their door.

He silently prayed that her mother would answer, but God chose to ignore this request.

The door opened, and Mr. Sherman filled the doorway, glaring down at him.

Jason stepped up onto the top step, so he didn't have to look up at the man. "I'm only here because I'm worried about Chevon."

"No need to be worried. She's not your concern."

"Is she here?"

He didn't answer.

"I've heard that you couldn't find her, and I think I have a right to know if she's still missing."

"A right?" the man shouted, and spit flew out of his mouth. He swore. "You don't have the right to anything, you arrogant little punk! Now get out of my sight!"

Jason focused on hiding his fear. Trying to be loud enough for Chevon to hear him, he said, "You're wrong."

Mr. Sherman barked out a laugh. "Oh, am I?" he roared. He stared at Jason as if expecting him to answer the question.

Jason didn't know what to say. It hadn't been a real question.

"What am I wrong about, exactly?" He inched closer as he spoke.

Still trying to be loud enough to be heard, Jason said, "You're wrong when you say she's not my concern. She is very much my concern. She is the mother of my child, and I love her." He hadn't meant to say it, and he tried to hide his surprise.

But he didn't have long to worry about that because Mr. Sherman grabbed him by the front of his jacket and shoved him backward. Jason hadn't been expecting the assault, and he flailed his arms for something to grab hold of, but his fingers only grazed the railing as he flew backward. His back slammed into the hard ground, knocking the wind out of him, and he heard Zoe's feet running. He was mortified. Some grown man he was. He'd been tossed off the porch like a rag doll, and now his female friend was running to his rescue.

"What is wrong with you?" Zoe nearly screamed. She sounded enraged, which further embarrassed him. She was acting like a mama bear, and he was her cub. "We can call the cops you know!"

The man roared with laughter. "Go ahead and call them." He slammed the door.

Zoe tried to help Jason up, but he shook her off. "Leave me alone."

She stepped back, obviously injured. "Fine." She turned and stomped back to the car.

Worried he might cry, Jason followed her, but then he heard the door open. His heart soared with hope that it would be Chevon, but he turned to see it was her mother.

She came running down the steps. "I'm so sorry, Jason. He's not like that. He's just so upset." She looked him up and down as if checking for injury. "Are you okay?"

"Yes." Physically, he was. In any other category, he was far from okay. He'd never been so humiliated.

She looked worriedly back at the door. "Please, don't call the police. He's not like that. Like I said, he's just scared." She looked Jason in the eye. "Please, Jason, if you care about Chevon, please let this go. This is a family matter, and we will take care of her. Please trust us to do what is best. I'm so glad to hear that you care about her, and when this all blows over, I will work to make sure that you're allowed to see her. But for now, you need to stay away and let us take care of our daughter." She reached out and squeezed his arm. "We have the appointment scheduled. This will all be over soon. I know you're a good kid, Jason. I know you're trying to do the right thing. But you're too young to know what the right thing is. Please let us handle it." She turned and hurried back to the house.

Feeling sick, Jason got into the car. "Well, this is the worst moment of my life."

"I'm so sorry."

"Me too. Me too." He turned around and headed out of the driveway, wishing he hadn't brought Zoe after all. This would have been embarrassing enough without extra witnesses. "Please don't tell anyone."

"I would never." She sounded horrified on his behalf, and her sympathy only deepened his shame.

"What am I going to do," he said aloud, not really meaning it to be a question.

She didn't answer.

"I need help."

Again, she said nothing, and he appreciated her silence. She didn't know how to help either.

He looked at the dashboard clock. "I wish I could talk to my dad, but he's working."

"We could go talk to Gramma."

The idea filled his heart with warmth. He didn't think she'd be able to help, but he knew her presence would make him feel better. He turned the car around. "Yes, let's go talk to Gramma."

Chapter 39

Esther

"What's the emergency?" Vicky looked around the sanctuary as if expecting to find the place ablaze. "I haven't even had my supper yet."

"We'll order a pizza," Rachel said.

Vicky gave Rachel a dirty look. "Oh, of course. Rachel knows what's going on." She looked at Esther. "What's the big secret?"

"There's no secret," Esther explained for the third time in the last five minutes. "But I only want to explain it once, and everybody isn't here yet." The truth was, she didn't want to put Jason through having to hear it explained more than once.

Vicky looked around the room. "Who's missing?"

Esther quickly took a mental roll call. "Just Vera and Pastor."

Vicky raised her eyebrows. "Oh? Pastor's coming? This must be serious."

Esther looked at Jason, who had his head in his hands. "It is serious, but there's nothing to worry about."

"If it's serious, then there's something to worry about." Vicky took off her coat and delicately eased herself into a chair. Zoe had helpfully made a circle of metal folding chairs. Esther hadn't thought all her invitees would fit into the upper room.

The front door opened, and Pastor Adam came inside. He looked around in wonder. "Wow. Quite a crowd."

"Thank you for coming, Pastor," Esther said.

"Of course. That's why you pay me the big bucks."

Lauren tittered, but no one else laughed.

Adam headed toward one of the empty chairs. "Okay, Sister, what's going on?" He was looking at Esther.

She didn't really want to be the one to fill everybody in, but she didn't know who else to tag with that task. She looked at the door, but Vera wasn't there yet. She took a deep breath. They would have to start without her. "Thank you, everyone, for coming. The kids came home early from school today because they needed some help—"

"What kids?" Vicky interrupted.

There were only two kids there, and Esther glanced at them. "Zoe and Jason."

"Oh, are they a couple now?" Vicky asked. "I can't keep track."

"No—" Esther started.

"Let her explain!" Barbara scolded.

Esther took a shaky breath. "Pastor, what you and a few of these others don't know is that Jason's friend Chevon is pregnant. She came to church with him last Sunday."

Adam was focusing on her words so carefully that he was making her nervous.

"Well, Jason ..." She wasn't sure how to say what she needed to say.

Jason sat up straight and took over. "Thank you, Esther. Let me try. I got Chevon pregnant, and I know that was wrong, but it happened, and now I would like to do the right thing."

Esther was proud of and impressed by Jason's boldness. She sneaked a look at the pastor, who wasn't trying to hide his surprise. Esther wished he would temper it a little.

"But Chevon's parents want her to get an abortion. I don't even know what Chevon wants. She changes her mind. A lot. But I think that if she had some time to really think about it, she would decide to keep the baby, but her parents aren't letting her. They are keeping her in the house, they have an appointment for the abortion, and they won't even let her talk to me on the phone."

No one moved nor spoke.

Jason leaned back in his chair. "That's pretty much the whole story. Now, everybody ... please tell me how to fix this."

Pastor exhaled slowly and looked around the circle. "Most of you don't look surprised."

"We're not," Barbara said.

"So you all know about this crisis, but no one thought to tell your pastor?"

"Sorry, Pastor," Esther said quickly. "I didn't really mean for the church to get this involved. It sort of just happened."

Pastor chuckled. "Yes, I think that's the way things are going to go for this church." He leaned forward and focused on Jason. "First of all, I applaud your character."

Jason looked shocked.

"That's a necessary first step in making this all work out."

Roderick, who sat beside Jason, patted his back. "That's right. You're being an upstanding man of God right now."

Jason looked doubtful.

"When is the appointment?" Pastor asked.

Jason shook his head. "I don't know."

"Well, they can't make her get an abortion against her will!" Barbara said as if that solved everything.

"No," Pastor said calmly, "but they could certainly pressure her into saying it's her will."

"So then what's the plan?" Barbara said.

Esther was almost amused at how invested Barbara was in this. But only almost.

"I'm thinking," Adam said.

"I know this isn't going to be a popular opinion," Walter said, and Esther stiffened. She wished he wouldn't give his unpopular opinion. "But why don't we just pray and other than that, stay out of it?"

Barbara gasped. "We can't stay out of it!"

"Sure we could. We pray about it but don't butt into their business anymore."

"I don't think anyone has butted into their business," Cathy said, looking around the circle. "Unless someone has done something I don't know about."

"I have," Rachel said.

Everybody looked at her expectantly.

"Of course you have," Vicky said.

Rachel chuckled. "I couldn't resist." Esther knew this wasn't true. Rachel had, in fact, tried to resist. And God had instructed her otherwise.

"I have a pretty good relationship with the girl," Rachel said, "and Jason's right. She is very confused. She told me herself that some moments she is excited to have a baby, but other moments she just wants to have an abortion."

Barbara gasped in horror.

Rachel glared at her. "I told you to stop being so judgmental. You have no idea what she's going through. She's doing great for a girl in her shoes. She doesn't even know the Lord, for crying out loud. She doesn't even know what's at stake here."

Barbara looked appropriately put in her place.

Pastor held up a hand. "Let's all calm down and try to treat each other with love. I know this is a heated topic, but we're not going to help anyone by bickering among ourselves."

Vera walked in then, looked around the room, and said, "What's going on?"

"I'll fill her in." Dawn got up from her chair and went to Vera.

The circle was quiet as the two women chatted by the doorway.

Cathy clicked her tongue. "I really have no idea what to do, Pastor. It's not like we can go kidnap her."

"No," Pastor said thoughtfully. "We sure can't."

"I don't think we would need to kidnap her," Jason said. "I think she would come willingly. But I can't get to her. I can't get into the house."

"And I don't think we should try to bust into their home," Cathy said. "Chevon is nearly an adult, but she's still a minor, and they are her parents."

"What if she wants to leave?" Barbara said. "If we knew that she wanted to leave, could the police help her get out?"

Everyone seemed to consider that idea.

But then Pastor said, "I'm not sure we should get the police involved."

"Why not?" Barbara cried.

Vera and Dawn joined the circle.

"We need to walk gently with meekness and love," Pastor said. "I don't think showing up with law enforcement will do that job."

Barbara rolled her eyes.

Pastor looked at Walter. "I think Walter had a good point."

"What?" Barbara cried.

"At this point, I can't think of anything else to do but pray. We're going to need God's help with this. So let's do that. Let's pray and ask him to give us a plan.

"We've *been* praying!" Barbara said. "We prayed together for an entire afternoon, and I've prayed a thousand times since."

"Good, good," Pastor said. "That means that God is already working this out. So let's keep praying. This is how we fight for that little one's life. With patience and humility. And while we're praying, God might tell us if there's something else he wants us to do. Or he might not tell us anything and do everything himself."

Jason looked disappointed.

Adam registered this. "I'm not saying that praying is all we're going to do, Jason. I'm just saying that it's all we're going to do right this second."

"You guys go ahead and pray," Vicky said. She stood up.

"You're leaving?" Dawn asked, sounding offended.

"Yes, but it's all right." She put her coat on. "I have a plan."

Everybody stared at her, waiting for her to elaborate.

"I'm not so sure any of us should be going off on our own," Lauren said gently.

Esther wasn't as concerned as Lauren, who hadn't known Vicky for very long. Esther had seen Vicky come through in a million different sticky situations. Vicky had a lot of wisdom contained within her sharp edges, and Esther knew that she often waited until it was desperately needed before she shared it. "Let's hear her out. What's your plan, Vicky?"

Vicky gave Esther an annoyed look. "Not that I'm obligated to share my plan with you. But first, I'm going to go have my supper. And then, I'm going to get a good night's sleep. And then, first thing tomorrow morning, I'm going in."

Chapter 40

Vicky

Vicky realized now that she had been a bit too cocky when she'd told her friends that she was going to get a good night's sleep. She had tossed and turned all night with occasional prayer spurts of varying lengths. A few times she had decided not to go through with this fool plan of hers and then had almost drifted off to sleep only to be awakened by her own conscience: *The God of comfort has comforted you so that you can comfort others.*

She was up before dawn drinking her coffee and reading her Bible when a bleary-eyed Emma staggered into the kitchen. Vicky looked up. "What are you doing up so early? You do know it's Saturday."

Emma rubbed her eye. "Early? I was coming for a midnight snack."

Vicky chortled. "Well, it's far past midnight, but go ahead and have your snack."

Emma opened the fridge and bent to look into it. "Something woke me up, and now I can't sleep. I always sleep better after some junk food."

"There are some Funny Bones in the pantry."

Emma stood up straight and closed the fridge. "Perfect! Thank you."

"Don't mention it." Vicky returned her eyes to her Bible, smiling. She had grown beyond fond of that child. Emma walked back by her, the cellophane crinkling in her hand. "Emma, promise me something."

She stopped and turned back toward Vicky. "Sure. What's up?"

"Promise me you will never be a pregnant teenager."

Emma wrinkled up her nose like a rabbit. "Eww. I promise."

Vicky smiled broadly. "That's my girl. Now go back to bed."

Emma disappeared into the shadows, and Vicky glanced at the clock. It was way too early to go visit the Shermans, unless she wanted to start off on an even worse note than she planned.

After a long shower she took her time getting dressed. Then she went back to her Bible for another hour or so. Finally, she couldn't stand it anymore. She told Tonya she was taking the car and then headed outside into the cold. It was her car, but they all shared it, so she didn't want to leave them stranded without warning them first.

Then she was on her way to the Shermans. She had gotten directions the night before from Esther, who was being surprisingly supportive of this. Esther had no way of knowing what Vicky was going to say to these people, and yet she trusted her. This trust gave Vicky confidence.

She'd also gotten a weird entertainment from the horror on some of the others' faces when she'd announced that she was getting involved. She chuckled now thinking about it. Maybe, when this was all said and done, she would make up some horrific story about how she stormed into their house screaming Scripture quotations and smashing everything with a golf club. Yes, yes, she would do that.

Her confidence waned as she pulled up the long driveway and then nearly vanished when she stopped in front of the neat little house. Father, if you want me to do this, you'd better equip me. She got out of the car, and her doubts vanished. This was exactly where she was supposed to be. God had been preparing her for this moment her whole life. She knocked on the door. No one came, and she feared they were going to ignore her. Or maybe they weren't home. She knocked again, and the door opened to reveal a tired-looking woman in a bathrobe.

"Good morning," Vicky said.

The woman recoiled a bit.

Vicky tried to smile. "May I speak with you and your husband? I'm Vicky." She wasn't sure what other information she could give. Anything else she could say would have little meaning for this woman. But she probably wasn't going to let her into her home based on the qualification of being Vicky.

"I'm a friend of Jason's."

Wrong choice. The woman stepped back and started to shut the door as she said, "I'm sorry. Now is not a good time."

Vicky put a hand on the door. "I'm afraid that what I have to say is time-sensitive."

"Look, my husband is sleeping, and if he finds you here, he is going to freak out, and it's going to be unpleasant for all of us. So please just go."

"I can be pretty unpleasant myself."

The woman looked at her curiously. "I'm sorry, but we've really had enough of church talk ... and religious talk ... and pro-life talk—"

"Wait. I'm not like them. I haven't come to tell you not to get an abortion."

Surprise registered on the woman's face, and she opened the door another few inches, betraying her curiosity.

"I've come to tell you what will happen if you do."

Chapter 41

Vicky

"Can I offer you some coffee?"

Vicky perched on the edge of the couch, not intending to stay long. "No, thank you. If you knew how much coffee I had already consumed this morning, you'd be horrified."

The woman chuckled. "I've been trying to set a record myself."

"I was young, unmarried," Vicky started. No use beating around the bush. "I was a bit of a wild child. Nothing like how wild an ordinary child is these days, but back then, I was considered to be living fast and loose."

The woman nodded understandingly.

"I had no excuse. I came from a good family, and when I got pregnant, I couldn't stand to embarrass them. So I went to talk to a man I knew, a man who could get things that people weren't allowed to get. And he told me where to go. And all alone, I went to a doctor's office." She shuddered remembering. It could hardly have been qualified as a doctor's office, even back then. "I can't even tell you how afraid I was of the place, of the procedure, and of the doctor himself. He was like a monster. That should tell you how afraid I was to have a baby out of wedlock. My fear of the abortion paled in comparison."

The woman started to say something, but Vicky didn't let her. "I'll spare you the details because I don't want to remember them too closely, but the pain of that day was nothing compared to the pain of all the days that followed. You see, less than a year later I met my husband, and less than a year after that we had our first child. Every day between the abortion and that delivery day, I thought of that little one I'd killed. Every single day I grieved him. I didn't want him, I got rid of him, and then I grieved him. And yet, I didn't wish I could go back and change things. Part of me still believed that I had done what I had to do. Part of me believed that I deserved that grief and that I deserved to suffer it for getting pregnant in the first place. I didn't yet have regrets." She took a big breath and straightened her blouse. "But then I met my daughter. Then I saw my baby in my arms and I realized what I had done, and the truth of it came smashing down on me like an anvil. It was a weight I couldn't tolerate. It destroyed me. I wanted to kill myself, but I couldn't because I now had this new small person to take care of.

"I loved that small person with all of my might. I was the best mom I could be. And every day of that child's life right up until now I've apologized to the baby that I killed. I ended up having three wonderful children, and it never got easier. I have never gotten over what I did. It hurts every second of every day. I know that God has forgiven me, and I have worked hard to forgive myself, but I can't. My husband doesn't know what I did. My kids don't know. My friends don't know. And I'm telling you now because I don't want what has happened to me to happen to your daughter."

The woman's eyes had grown wider as Vicky talked, and this had encouraged Vicky to keep going. Now she sat speechless.

"That's all I had to say. I will get out of your hair now." She stood to go.

"I don't know what to say."

"You don't have to say anything. But I beg you to consider what I've shared." It was not easy to share it, she thought. Please don't let me have done so in vain.

"I just never thought about it like that. I thought women just moved on."

"Women do move on because they are women, and they have to. But it never stops hurting."

The woman nodded soberly. "I'm not sure what I think of any of this, but I thank you for sharing your story."

"You're welcome, and now I ask you not to share it with anyone else unless you decide your daughter needs to hear it."

"Of course."

Vicky showed herself out and made it all the way to the end of the driveway before the tears came.

Chapter 42

Chevon

Chevon knew there was a strange woman in the house, but she didn't know who she was, and she didn't care. She could hear her voice, and she knew she wasn't Rachel or Esther, so what did it matter?

In the past, on occasion, Chevon had thought she was feeling depressed. Now she knew that had not been depression. This was.

She was a prisoner in her house, and her parents were the wardens. She had no say about what happened in her own life. Of course it had always been this way, but the stakes had never been this high. If she was old enough to have sex, get pregnant, and have a baby, then she was old enough to make a decision about whether to have the baby. She could hear her father's voice in her head, countering this argument: "You aren't old enough to have sex, get pregnant, and have a baby."

Not having her phone made her feel like she was missing a part of her body. She was constantly reaching for it, looking for it, wanting to look at it. She didn't even miss her friends, except for maybe Jason. She just missed the ability to be able to check in with them. Her prison sentence would be going by much faster if she had some social media to scroll through.

She rolled over and flung her arm over her head. What Jason must be thinking now. It was killing her that her father had hurt him. But what a complete and utter doofus, he was, showing up like that and declaring his love for her to her father. She shook her head while remembering. What had he been thinking?

And was it true? Or was he just trying to play honorable for her father? She thought it was probably the latter. He had shown no signs of loving her, ever. As a matter of fact, she'd never seen him show any signs of loving anyone.

"Why did you let her in?" her father bellowed. Oh. Dad was awake. He'd been sleeping in because he'd spent half the night patrolling the hallway outside her bedroom. He had literally nailed her window shut and then he'd made sure she didn't sneak out through the door.

What was going to happen on Monday? Were they going to drag her down the stairs and outside, and then force her into the car? Were they going to drag her into the clinic? Just what exactly was their plan? The clinic wasn't out in the middle of the woods somewhere. It was in the middle of Ellsworth. There would be witnesses, watching her scream and try to wrestle out of their grasp. And if they thought she was going to do anything differently, they didn't know her as well as they thought. She wasn't as committed to having this baby as she was to defying their attempt to completely control her life.

"What did you just say?" he hollered. She hadn't heard her mother answer, but her father's voice carried. "How stupid can you be?"

She sat up. He didn't usually talk to her mother like that. No, correction, he didn't *ever* talk to her mother like that. She didn't think her mother was going to appreciate it.

Her father was losing his mind. Sure, it wasn't great that his daughter was a pregnant teen, but did it really justify this level of insanity?

"Don't get sucked into Chevon's drama," he hollered. "You've been rock steady ..." She missed the second half of that sentence, got up, and pressed her ear to the door. "... use your common sense!"

She could hear her mother talking, but she couldn't make out the words. She was talking quickly, and she sounded really upset. Obviously. Her husband had just called her stupid.

He started swearing, and his voice grew louder. Chevon backed away from the door, fearing he was coming to holler at her some more. She looked at the window hopelessly. Maybe she could just smash it. She looked around her room for something heavy. But then he was knocking on the door. She ran and jumped into the bed and pulled the covers over her head. She heard the door open, and she concentrated on breathing slowly. He stood there for what felt like a year and then the door clicked shut again. She sighed in relief, and tears flooded out of her. How had things gotten this messed up? She longed for Jason. She wanted to feel his arms around her. She wanted him to tell her it was all going to be okay. The tears came harder and faster, and as she tried to keep her crying quiet, she cried herself to sleep.

Chapter 43

Chevon

Chevon woke to her arm being shaken. Disorientated, she scrambled away from whoever was touching her and sat up. Brilliant sunlight streamed in through her window. She rubbed her eyes. She'd fallen asleep during the day? Then she remembered. She had cried herself to sleep. She looked at her mother, who had been doing some crying of her own. "What?"

"Do you want to get out of here?"

Chevon looked at the open bedroom door. "What?"

"Your father went to the store. We don't have much time. If you want to get out of here, I will get you out."

Chevon nodded and jumped out of bed. She jammed her feet into her sneakers, and without even pulling the heels up, clomp-clomped toward the stairs.

"Don't you want to pack a bag?"

Chevon looked back. "What, are we leaving forever?"

Her mother just stood there, looking confused. "I don't know what we're doing."

This scared Chevon a little. Her mother always had a plan. She always had a destination, a reason to head that way, and a series of steps to take.

The woman looking at her now had none of those things.

Chevon went back into her room, grabbed a backpack, and started shoving random things into it.

"I'll meet you at the door."

Chevon was further disheartened to see that her mother had packed a bag of her own. She ran down the stairs. What was going on? Was her mother leaving her father? "Do you want to stay here? You could say I snuck out." Guilt seemed to be coming at Chevon from all angles.

Her mother shook her head. "I need to get away from him."

Chevon stepped outside as her mother shut the door behind them.

"You mean for good?"

Her mom gave her a look that she'd given her a billion times before. Good. Her mother was still there. "Of course not. Don't be ridiculous. People can fight without getting a divorce."

Chevon got into the car and buckled up. "Where are we going?"

Her mom sped out of the driveway. She didn't answer the question.

"Mom?"

"I'm not sure. I was trying to think of a friend, but if I tell one of my friends how your father has been acting, it'll be all over town in an hour. And no offense, but I don't really want to be discussing my pregnant teen with anyone, even if they all do already know about it." She sighed. "I wish we could go to Gramma's but it's too far, and I don't have enough money to get there—"

"I don't want to get too far away from Jason anyway."

Her mother rolled her eyes. "Oh please. He is the least of my worries right now."

"Well, he's one of my worries. He's a pretty big piece of this puzzle, Mom."

"I don't want him anywhere near your puzzle, Chevon."

Chevon's heart sank. She thought her mother had been coming around. "I thought you were starting to understand."

"I am." She took a long breath. "I'm not so sure that we should be forcing you to get an abortion, but that doesn't mean you're going to marry Jason DeGrave. Chevon, you're only sixteen. You shouldn't be picking out your husband now. That's a recipe for disaster. A recipe for divorce. You don't even know who you are yet."

Well, *that* was incredibly patronizing. "I know exactly who I am. *You* don't know who I am."

"Chevon, that's not fair." She stomped on the gas, and Chevon feared she was really going to leave town.

She scanned her brain, trying to think of somewhere they could go. "We could go to Bucksport and get a hotel room? Just hide out for a bit while we figure things out."

"That's not a bad idea, but your father would see the charge on the credit card."

She leaned back and turned her head toward her mom. "Can we just go to Jason's?"

"Stop it! This is confusing enough without involving your feelings for him!" Her mom looked at her. "And where did these feelings even come from anyway? Have you been pining away for him for a long time? I thought you had more sense!"

"What's wrong with Jason?"

She tightened her grip on the wheel. "Nothing's wrong with Jason. He's just a small boy from a small town, and I had bigger hopes for you."

"He's a good man." It felt so strange calling him a man, but she certainly wasn't going to call him a boy. "What about Rachel's house?"

Her mom chewed her lip. "That's not a terrible idea."

She waited for her to say more. "So? Is that where we're going?"

"I think that he would think to look there."

That was a good point. That would probably be the first place he would check. "Wait! Isn't that Rachel's car right there?" She pointed.

Her mom looked out her window. "Is this that church?"

"Yes! Slow down."

"Oh my goodness."

"What?"

"That's Vicky right there."

Who was Vicky?

She pulled the car over to the curb but didn't shut it off. "What are they doing?"

Women were coming out of the church carrying boxes and putting them into someone's trunk. As they watched, one of them shut the trunk, and the car left. A truck took its place, and the women started placing boxes into its bed.

"Are those food boxes?" her mom asked.

What did it matter? "We should go inside."

"We can't just go walking in. We don't even know what's going on."

"Of course we can go walking in. It's a church." Her mom didn't seem to understand this principle. "Come on, Mom. If we just sit here, he will drive by and see us."

Her mom gasped and pulled her phone out of her purse. "We need to shut our phones off or he can track them."

"I don't have a phone anymore," Chevon said angrily.

Her mom ignored her. She stared at the phone screen until it went black and then tucked it back into her purse. She looked up at the church and sighed. "Okay, I guess we go in because I don't know where else to go. But only on one condition."

"Name it."

"If I say we're leaving, don't fight me on it. I know you think you're an adult, and you almost are. But I still know more about this world and how it works than you do, and I need you to trust me. I've done right by you for sixteen years. I'm not going to fail you now." She reached out and cupped her chin. "I need you to trust me like you've always trusted me, and if I say we're leaving, then I have a reason, and we need to leave. Okay?"

Chevon nodded, her eyes threatening to spout more tears. She loved her mother so much and didn't think she'd ever needed her more desperately.

"I love you so much, and I am really on your side with this, but work with me, okay? Not against me."

Chevon nodded. She was so comforted to hear these words. She had been needing to hear them for weeks.

Chapter 44

Esther

Esther was working so hard that sweat ran down her temples. Finding this most unseemly, she asked sweet Mary Sue to take over her box-packing station so she could go turn the heat down. It would have been easier to just ask Mary Sue to deal with the thermostat, but she also wanted a break from the work.

She reached the top of the stairs just in time to see Chevon step inside with her mother. "Hallelujah," she said aloud.

Adam heard the outburst of praise and looked at her curiously. Then he followed her gaze toward the door.

"That's them," she whispered.

"Awesome!" He headed that way.

She followed, wishing they hadn't shown up right in the middle of chaotic food distribution. But that's when God had sent them, so Esther would be content with it. Maybe they needed food.

"Welcome!" Adam said warmly with what Esther thought to be an appropriate amount of enthusiasm. She knew he was showing restraint, and she thought that was wise. Despite her admiration and appreciation for the man, she didn't quite yet trust him to run the show, so she watched him closely.

Mary Sherman looked terrified. It was clear that both women had been crying, but Chevon looked significantly more stable than her mother.

Mary looked around the sanctuary, her eyes lingering on the high ceiling. "This place is quite beautiful."

"Thank you," Adam said. "Though I really can't take the credit."

Mary tried to smile but couldn't quite pull it off.

"Would you like some food?" Esther asked.

Mary shook her head quickly. "No, no ..." She looked at Chevon.

Chevon looked at Esther. "We had some drama at my house this morning. My dad is pretty upset." She held up a hand. "Not like violent upset or anything. He's not dangerous. We just wanted a place to lay low while we try to figure out what to do."

"Of course, of course," Esther said.

"Would you like to have a seat?" Adam asked.

"Actually, maybe we should give them the upper room? It might be more comfortable." And more private.

"Why don't we show them the way, and they can decide," Adam said. "We don't want them to feel trapped or anything." He laughed goofily. "But you're welcome to stay as long as you want."

"Right this way." Esther headed for the stairs.

They met Rachel halfway up.

"Hello!" Rachel cried, ecstatic to see them. She turned and headed back up the stairs and was the first into the upper room. She swept her arm across the room. "Come on in. Make yourself comfortable."

Chevon and Mary sat, Mary looking distinctly *un*comfortable.

"Can we get you anything?" Rachel said. "Some coffee?"

Esther wasn't sure they even had any coffee made. She hadn't made any, so it probably hadn't been done.

"Coffee would be great," Mary said.

Chevon pointed at her belly. "I don't think I'm supposed to have caffeine."

Her mother gave her an irritated look.

Esther realized that Rachel was staring at her expectantly. What, she was waiting for *her* to go get the cup of coffee? But she was the one who'd offered it! But Rachel was such a busybody that she didn't want to leave the room. Esther tried to avoid her eyes.

Apparently Adam read the situation, and apparently he didn't want to go fetch the coffee either because he said, "I'll text Lauren, ask her to bring some up."

Mary looked up at him. "Could you ask Vicky to bring it?"

Esther hoped that the surprise on her face wasn't as obvious as the shock on Rachel's and Adam's.

"I don't think Vicky would get a text anytime in the near future, but I'll ask Lauren to bring her along."

Chevon looked at Esther. "I don't have a phone, but can you get in touch with Jason? I want him to know I'm okay and that I'm here."

Again, her mother looked irritated.

Esther didn't know what was going on here, but it was obvious they still had some issues to work through. Esther didn't have her phone with her so she couldn't text or call Jason. It seemed she would have to leave the room after all. "I'll go ask Zoe to let him know. I'll be right back." She hustled down the stairs, got frustrated when she couldn't find Zoe, and finally found her outside carrying boxes.

"Chevon and her mother just came in."

Zoe stopped moving, and her mouth fell open. "Seriously?"

As if Esther would make that up. "Yes, seriously," she said impatiently. "Chevon doesn't have her phone, but she wants Jason to know that she's here and that she's all right. Can you let him know?"

"Of course." Zoe put the box down right where she stood and took out her phone.

"You can finish delivering the box first."

Zoe looked at the line of cars. "They've been waiting a while. Another thirty seconds won't hurt." Her brow furrowed in concentration, she started stabbing at her screen with both thumbs.

Having accomplished her mission, Esther hurried back into the church and up the stairs. Rachel and Adam had sat on either side of the women, and Lauren and Vicky had joined them. Miracle of miracles, Mary now held a cup of coffee in her hand.

Esther felt left out and then felt guilty for feeling left out. This isn't about you, she tried to remind herself.

"Well, believe it or not," Adam said, "I can understand why you would feel that way about Christianity."

Vicky visibly bristled.

"Christians are only human, and they misbehave a lot. That misbehavior is harder to ignore when they're judging others at the same time as they're acting like idiots."

A small smile crept onto Mary's face.

"But regardless of how you feel about religion, this building is a safe place for you. And these people are a safe place for you. And if any of them ever act stupid, just try to remember that they're human too, and they're doing the best they can."

Mary nodded and then looked down at her hands.

"Would you like me to reach out to your husband? I would be happy to talk to him."

Chevon's eyes grew wide.

Her mother shook her head.

"I wouldn't try to talk him into or out of anything," Adam added. "I would mostly just listen."

Mary seemed to be considering it.

"You know what? Why don't you think about it, and let me know if you'd like me to do that." Adam looked around the room. "Why don't we clear out for a minute, give them some time to relax and chat." He stood up.

Esther didn't like this one bit. She didn't even know what they were doing here! She didn't know the plan! She'd missed everything!

"Actually," Mary said weakly. "Can Vicky stay?"

Again, most jaws in the room dropped.

Vicky, who had started to get up, sat back down.

Mary looked at the older woman. "I was hoping you could talk to my daughter."

Chapter 45

Chevon

W hen Chevon heard Jason's voice on the stairs, a thrill danced through her belly. She was disgusted with how excited she was to see him, but she couldn't help it. And then when he came into view, her excitement doubled. It was all she could do not to leap up and run into his arms. She could hardly believe it. Jason DeGrave. She'd known him for so long, been irritated by him for so long, had rolled her eyes at all the other girls fawning over him for so long. Yet here she was.

But all of that felt like a million years ago. So much had changed.

She looked at her mother, hoping she wouldn't be too cruel, and her face was impassive. Good, that was better than mean.

"Well, hello, superstar," Vicky said, and Chevon didn't know if she was being sarcastic or not.

"What happened?"

"Not much," Chevon answered quickly so her mother wouldn't. "My dad is just really mad, so we wanted to take a break."

As if Jason wasn't there, her mother looked at her. "I could support having the baby and giving it up for adoption."

The grimace on Jason's face made Chevon love him even more.

"I think I could get your father to go along with that—"

"Mom, that's impossible."

Her mom looked at her. "Honey, I'm really trying here."

"I know you are," Chevon said quickly. "And I appreciate it. But I'm not giving a baby up for adoption. Have you even met me? I can't let go of an old doll."

Despite the hefty cloak of emotions her mother was bearing, she laughed at this. Then she put her head in her hands. "Then I don't know what to do. If abortion isn't an option, and adoption isn't an option, and my teenager having a baby isn't an option, then what does that leave us with?"

"Feel free to ignore my input," Vicky said, "but maybe your teenager just has to grow up a little."

Chevon jerked back. How patronizing could she be?

Vicky gave her a gentle look. "Take it easy. You're a great sixteen-year-old. But you've got to grow up a few years in the next nine months, so that by the time this baby is living outside of you, you are mature enough to be a mother."

Her mother was gazing at her as if wondering if that was possible.

"I can do it, Mom. I really think I can."

The sadness in her mother's eyes nearly broke her heart. "Chevon, maybe we shouldn't have come here. I don't know how to advise you, and now I brought you to a place where everybody is advising you in only one direction."

"Mom, it's the right direction! And I don't even care if it's right or wrong. It's what I want." Did she want to be a mother right this second? No, definitely not. But would it still be a happy, fulfilling use of her life? She thought so.

"I hate to interrupt," Jason said, and Chevon knew that wasn't true. Jason loved having the floor. "But can I talk to Chevon alone for a minute?"

Chevon stood up without asking her mother for permission. Her mother reached up and grabbed her hand but then she looked at Jason. "You're not leaving the building, are you?"

Jason shook his head. "Definitely not."

Her mother let go of her.

She followed Jason down the stairs, across the sanctuary, and down another set of stairs into a busy basement.

"Whoops, I didn't know there would be this many people here." Jason led her to an empty corner. He dragged two chairs over and sat in one of them.

She sat facing him, and he took her hand.

"I have so much to say to you," he started, "and I'm terrified to say any of it. I have really strong feelings for you, and I don't really understand them, so I'm scared to share them because what if I'm wrong about them?"

He was butchering this, but she appreciated his effort.

"I'm pretty sure I'm in love with you. But what do I know, right? I'm just a stupid teenage boy. But I know that I care an awful lot. So I'd like to try to be your man. And if it doesn't work out, I will still be our child's father. But I'd like to try for it to work out."

She was speechless.

"I'm out on the end of a limb here, and I'm kinda freaking out. You should say something."

She giggled. Self-consciously she looked at the others in the room. None of them were looking at her, but she still felt them paying attention. "I'm pretty confused too, and I do not want to admit to having feelings for Jason DeGrave." She giggled. "All my life I've tried not to be like everybody else, but here I am."

He shook his head quickly. "I'm not the same guy that those girls had crushes on. Not even close."

She studied him. "That's a good point. And I didn't have feelings for you a few months ago." She felt her cheeks get hot. "Well, actually, I guess that's when they started."

His cheeks got pink too, which made her feel better.

"Do you want to try a relationship with me?"

She nodded. "Sure."

"Do you want to have a baby with me?"

She gulped. This was all getting so real. She did want to have a baby with him, didn't she? But could she? Could she really be a mother? She wished she had more time to decide. A few days. A few weeks, even. But the appointment was Monday. "Not sure yet."

Chapter 46

Jason

D espite everything, Jason's head was in the clouds. He wanted to grab Chevon, squeeze her tight, and kiss her tenderly. Of course, he did none of this. This new relationship had turned him into such a wuss.

Someone shouted upstairs, and the color drained from Chevon's face. "My father's here," she breathed.

"Really? That didn't sound like him."

"It wasn't, but he's here."

Why did she think that? Jason wished he'd gotten a more definite answer from her before her father showed up, but if the man really was there, Jason didn't want to be hiding in the basement. "Come on. Let's go see." He took her hand, and they started across the room. Half the people who'd been packing boxes had stopped and were looking at the ceiling. Several others were already on their way up the stairs to see what the commotion was.

The closer Jason got, the more the shouting intensified. Multiple voices now, and he didn't recognize any of them.

When they reached the sanctuary, Chevon immediately ducked behind the projector screen. He followed her, not because he wanted to hide, but because he wanted to keep her close.

There were several loud, angry men in the sanctuary, but none of them were Chevon's father. Jason sighed in relief. But whoever the men were, they were causing just as much trouble as her father would have. Officer Pettiford was on the scene and trying to help Pastor Adam get the men back out of the church.

Judith Puddy started crying and ran toward Lauren, who scooped her up and headed toward the basement stairs. Anger surged through Jason. The power of it scared him a little. He peeked around the screen to get a better look at the scene.

Oblivious to the fact that they'd just scared a child, the men got even louder. One of them got right in Pastor Adam's face. "You have no right!" he screamed. "Who do you think you are?"

"Sir," Officer Pettiford said. "If we could please take this outside."

Another man shouted, "We'll take it outside as soon as you let her go!"

Let who go? Chevon?

The man in Pastor's face swore and threatened him, but Pastor didn't even flinch, making Jason wonder how often the man got screamed at. Jason, having suffered a long line of terrible coaches, had been screamed at a lot and knew that he wouldn't be handling it as well as Adam was.

The door opened.

"Your dad's here," Jason whispered.

Chevon closed her eyes.

Officer Pettiford raised his voice, demanding they all go back outside.

They still didn't move.

He threatened to start cuffing people, and they slowly edged toward the door.

"Are they talking about me?" she whispered. "Do they mean let *me* go?"

He didn't know. That didn't make any sense. He watched the last man go outside, and then he gently tugged her in that direction. Vicky and Mrs. Sherman came out of the stairwell wide-eyed. Mrs. Sherman looked at her daughter. "Was that your dad?"

Chevon nodded.

Jason continued toward the door, and Chevon followed. There was no window handy to look out, so Jason opened the door and then wished he hadn't. The lawn was full. Who were all these people? Only a few of them were shouting, and two more police officers were trying to deal with those people. Most of the people were just standing around.

After a moment, Jason realized that a lot of the gawkers had been waiting in line for food and had simply gotten out of their cars. So they hadn't come special just to protest his life. What a relief.

Still holding his hand, Chevon stepped closer to him and wrapped her other hand in the crook of his arm. He let go of her hand so he could put his arm around her. Mrs. Sherman flanked her daughter on the other side, and Vicky protectively stepped in front of all three of them. "Oh, for Pete's sake," Vicky said. "How can people even be this stupid?"

Pastor Adam came back up the steps, gave Jason a reassuring smile, and then turned to face the growing crowd. New cars were pulling over, and new onlookers were spilling out. Adam raised his hands. "Welcome to New Beginnings Church!" he announced with a joy that sounded completely sincere.

This time Jason did laugh.

So did Vicky. "Nice touch," she said.

"We have been blessed with an abundance of food and household supplies here, and we are giving away boxes of that blessing to anyone who wants some." Pastor pointed toward the line of now empty cars. "If you'd like a box or two of goodies, go ahead and line up right over there. If you are here for any other reason, I respectfully ask you to remain civil and kind. You are of course welcome to hang out on New Beginnings' lawn, but I would ask you not to shout at or threaten any of the people here."

"Religious nut!" a man shouted.

One of the original bullies shouted at Officer Pettiford, "We'll start being civil when you make them let her go!"

Another of the originals turned toward the crowd and yelled, "This cult is holding a teenage girl against her will!"

Chevon stiffened beside him.

A collective gasp came from the lawn, and several people started shouting. "What?" "That's illegal!" "Get her out!"

A woman who had only just arrived marched up to one of the police officers and screamed, "Why aren't you doing anything?"

Adam held up his hands again. "Please!" he shouted, still somehow managing to sound joyful. "We are not holding anyone here. Anyone here is free to leave at any time."

Interesting that he didn't mention that they weren't a cult. Jason wished he had. Oh no. Alita's car stopped up the street, and she jumped out. Of course. He looked at Mrs. Sherman. "Should we get Chevon somewhere else?"

She was so pale that she looked ill.

"No," Vicky answered for her. "This is the best place for them to be." She opened the door. "Though we might want to go back inside. These lunatics will drift off eventually."

Chapter 47

Esther

Wanting to avoid whatever was happening at the front door, Esther had gone out the back. At first she tried to be sneaky as she came around the building, but then she realized that there were so many people there that no one was going to pay her any mind. Her heart sank as more and more of the crowd came into view. There had to be nearly a hundred people there. She wanted a crowded New Beginnings but not like this.

"Cult! Cult! Cult!" people chanted. Where had that accusation come from? It didn't even make sense!

"This isn't a cult!" Derek shouted. He stood only a few feet away from her. He looked wild with anger, and she feared what he might do. He could be erratic *without* cause.

Esther scanned the crowd for her granddaughter's face and found her near the line of cars, a food box still in her arms. Her mouth hung open.

Movement on the front steps drew Esther's eyes, and she looked in time to see Vicky usher Mary back inside. Vicky tried to get Chevon to go too, but the young woman wouldn't move. She stood resolute, glaring out at the crowd. Esther followed her gaze to see her ire was aimed at her father.

Carl Pettiford scaled the steps and stood beside Pastor. "Attention!" he shouted. "This has become an unsafe situation! I am ordering you all to disperse peacefully, or we will start making arrests!"

Adam started to protest, but Carl shut him down. "We are taking charge—"

"Fascists!" a woman screamed. Esther knew her. She'd been in Christy's class growing up.

Carl looked bewildered as someone else echoed her insult.

"Yeah! Fascists!" a man shouted.

Carl squeezed the microphone on his radio and spoke rapidly. Of course, Esther had no idea what he'd said, but she hoped he was calling for backup. Lots of it.

"This church is trying to force a child to have a baby!" Christy's former classmate screamed. "And the fascist cops are backing them!"

This is going to be on the news, Esther thought and nearly wept. Her beloved church. The whole state was going to think they were a bunch of nuts.

More people joined in the shouting as neighbors drifted out of their houses and wandered toward the chaos. Esther's heart raced with fear. Pastor Adam had started out doing a great job handling this, but now he stood silent. Were the police helping or making it worse? She didn't know. She didn't know what to do. She started to pray fervently.

Carl nodded to another officer who ordered one of the men to put his hands behind his back. Esther expected this to calm the crowd a bit, but it had the opposite effect. Someone shoved the officer. He staggered sideways, got his footing, and then reached toward his weapon. He didn't draw it, but people backed up as if he had, managing to look both terrified and angry. They kept shouting. "Women have rights!" "Let her go!" "Get her out!"

"Disperse, now!" Carl shouted. He was impressively loud, but not loud enough. He put his hand on his weapon. Probably just for show, Esther thought, but it still scared her. Carl shouted orders, but he could barely be heard over the din.

And then rising above the chaos came a piercing shriek. It took Esther a few seconds to recognize its source.

Chevon.

Her mouth was open, her throat tight, as she screamed at the top of her lungs. She wasn't saying a word. She was just screaming. And it worked. The crowd fell silent. The scream stopped, and even from as far away as Esther was, she could see the girl was trembling from head to toe. "I am the girl!" she shouted. "Most of you know me! I am pregnant! This church is helping me. They are not a stupid cult!" She sucked in a lungful of air and then bellowed, "My dad is trying to force me to have an abortion." There was another collective gasp. "No!" she screamed. "Don't you dare gasp at that! Don't you dare gasp at any of this! This is none of your business! This is not a political issue. This is my life. This is my baby's life. Would you please all go home! This is my choice, and I'm going to make it!" She looked at Jason. He stood tall, his shoulders back, his jaw tight. He gave her the slightest nod, and she turned back to the crowd. "And I'm choosing to have this baby! I'm going to be a mother!" She stopped, and her voice echoed back to her. That was the only response she received as the whole town stared at her.

"No," she said more quietly. There was no need to shout anymore. "I already am a mother." With her chin high, she turned and went inside.

Jason followed her.

Carl turned to face the crowd. "You heard her. There's nothing criminal going on here—yet. Disperse now, or there will be arrests. State Troopers are on their way."

Looking disappointed, most of the people started to drift away. Those who remained stayed disgruntled but silent. It seemed there was nothing left for them to fight about.

Chapter 48

Chevon

When Chevon's father came into the room, she sat up straight on instinct. Then she regretted it. She didn't want him to think she was afraid of him. To that end, she kept her eyes focused on the television.

This didn't last long, though, as he used an app on his phone to pause her show. Still, she avoided eye contact.

He sat on the ottoman. "Chevon, look at me." His voice was still gruff, but he wasn't shouting.

She swung her eyes toward him, and instantly they filled with tears. She looked away again, wishing she could control the spigot even a little. Then she felt guilty and forced herself to look at him again.

His eyes were soft and wet. He'd been doing some weeping himself, it seemed.

"I'm sorry," she said before she realized she was going to.

He raised an eyebrow. "Are you?"

She scowled. "Of course I am! Are you crazy?"

He straightened his upper back and studied her. "Try to see this from my point of view. I'm your father. I am desperate to protect you. All your life, when you've had a problem, I've tried to fix it. And I ... and you ... why won't you let me fix this one?"

She didn't know what to say to that.

"Why are you being so stubborn?"

She knew where she got her stubbornness, but she bit her tongue.

"I'm trying to understand, honey. I really am. I thought I knew you. I've known you your whole life ..." He closed his eyes and exhaled. "And I never saw this coming." He seemed to realize what he'd said and held up both hands. "Obviously I knew that boys were coming. If I hadn't, I *would* be crazy. But I didn't know *this* was coming. I never expected you to want to be a teen mom."

"I don't *want* to be a teen mom, Dad," she said, her exasperation coming through loud and clear.

"Is that so? Because you just stood on some church steps and declared to the whole town that you do." The anger was creeping back into his voice. Or was that embarrassment?

Maybe both.

"I didn't *mean* to get pregnant. But now that I am, there's really only two options. And I don't like either of them. But one of them ..." She really wanted him to understand. "And I've figured out that one of them really isn't an option at all."

He raised his eyebrows. "And did you figure that out because a bunch of religious nuts convinced you it was *sinful*?" He coated the word with irony.

She shook her head. "They didn't convince me of anything. I don't want to kill my baby." Saying it aloud to him strengthened her resolve.

He studied her for so long that she grew restless under his gaze. Then he exhaled loudly. "I really wish you weren't pregnant. I really wish you hadn't stood on a church's porch and screamed your lungs out. I really wish you hadn't defied me in front of the whole town.

But seeing you up there ... seeing how strong you're being through all of this, well ..." He paused for so long she wondered if he was finished. "I'm not proud that you're pregnant, but I was proud of your strength back there." A tear slipped out of his eye. "With that said, you've got time to change your mind—"

"I won't."

He narrowed his eyes. "Don't interrupt me, especially when I'm working so hard to see your side of this."

He was? "Sorry," she mumbled.

He nodded. "If you do change your mind, I want you to come to me." He paused. "Can you at least promise me that?"

She nodded.

"Thank you. I don't want you to feel trapped. You're not trapped. Not yet. But ..." He folded his arms across his chest. "But I guess I can't *make* you have an abortion. So I'm not saying that I support this, and I definitely don't support Jason DeGrave, but I do support *you*." His voice cracked. "You are my daughter, and I love and support you even when I don't understand you. I guess I've got to accept that you're an adult now. Sort of."

She couldn't believe what she was hearing. She couldn't wait to tell Jason. "Thank you," she whispered.

"You're welcome. This doesn't mean that I'm happy. But nothing you can ever do will make me stop loving you. You will never stop being my daughter." He stared at her.

She didn't know what he wanted her to say, so she said, "Thank you," again.

"You're welcome," he said again. Then he smiled, and it was almost as if he was back to being her old dad again. "Now give me a few days before we talk about it again, okay?" He stood and turned to go. Then he turned back. "Unless you change your mind. In that case, come to me right away. But otherwise, can you take a few days off from Jason and that church?" He swore. "I need a break from all that too."

Again she didn't know what to say. "I guess."

He shook his head and smiled. "Never a dull moment with you, kiddo."

Chapter 49

Zoe

Z oe went through the motions of her team's warm-ups singing along with the music. She'd learned the drills by now and didn't have to concentrate as much on where to run when. Now she only had to focus when it was time to shoot. She took a long breath, grateful she wasn't as nervous as she used to be. This was her fifth game. Part of her couldn't wait for the season to be over so she could stop running and give the blisters on her heels time to heal. Part of her was loving basketball. Though she was never going to admit that to Jason.

She stopped at the end of the layup line and caught Levi looking at her. She smiled at him, and he looked surprised. This made her feel guilty. Why was he surprised by a smile? Suddenly the ball was right in her face. She got her hands up just in time. It almost smashed her in the nose, and that would've been quite embarrassing with Levi looking right at her. She threw it to the next girl and then ran for the hoop.

The drill was to catch a bounce pass and then go up for a layup, but Coach made her catch the ball, plant her feet, and then shoot. She was the only one instructed to do this drill incorrectly. She wasn't sure if she should feel embarrassed or special.

After a few minutes of free shooting, which Zoe spent directly under the hoop, the buzzer sounded, and they all ran to the bench.

Coach Hodges rattled off the starters, and Zoe almost keeled over dead when she heard her name.

"Yeah!" Callie slapped her on the back. "Way to go, Zoe!"

Zoe smiled at her and mouthed, "Thanks."

"I need you to really guard number thirty-three." Coach looked at her intently. "Just like we practiced."

Thirty-three was the other team's version of Zoe. She was the tallest player they'd faced. Zoe nodded. She would do it. She could do it. She would keep that girl from getting the ball.

Her teammates got out of the way so the starters could sit, and now she was nervous again.

She met Levi's eyes, and he shot a fist into the air, grinning ear to ear. She smiled back, and this time he didn't look so surprised. She couldn't wait to talk to him about this. She knew he would poke fun at her being a big-time jock now, and she couldn't wait.

They called her name, and her chest swelled with pride as she ran out to shake the opposing athlete's hand. She clapped as her other teammates were announced, and then they lined up for the national anthem. Her leg bounced nervously up and down for what felt like the longest song in history.

And then she was out on the floor for tipoff. She was so nervous she felt sick. Was she really going to throw up on the basketball court? If she did, she would have to move back to Missouri.

"Zoe, take it!"

Take what? She looked at her coach and saw her pointing at the circle in the middle of the court. What? She panicked. She didn't know how to do tipoff! They'd never practiced that.

"Don't worry," Callie whispered in her ear. "You've got this. Just keep your eye on the ball and try to tap it to me. No big deal if you don't."

It felt like someone else's legs that carried her to that circle. Zoe looked her opponent up and down. Zoe was a hair taller, but Coach had said that this girl knew what she was doing. Zoe silently prayed. *If you care about basketball, help me do this.* Then she hoped that the other girl wasn't praying the same. The ref blew the whistle and tossed the ball up in the air. What? No! She wasn't ready. She jumped, tried to tap the ball—and missed it completely.

The other team took off in the other direction and a very embarrassed Zoe turned to chase the ball. She'd only gone a few steps when the other team scored.

She wanted to die. She hoped Coach would take her out. How does someone miss the ball completely? She was probably the first person in history to do that. She turned to trudge down the court, and Levi's voice rose above the crowd.

"Way to go, Zoe! You're a rock star!"

Her heart swung from grief to glory in the course of that sentence. She got into position, sealed the defender just like Coach had taught her, and spread her arms wide for the ball. Callie hit her in the perfect spot, and the ball did not smash into her nose. Zoe caught it as if she had done it hundreds of times before, pivoted, and shot. The ball went through the hoop, and the whistle blew. For a second, Zoe panicked, not sure what she'd done wrong. But then her teammates were slapping her on the back and congratulating her, and she realized that the tall girl had fouled her.

"You have to shoot a foul shot now," Callie whispered.

Oh no. Her foul shot average in practice was less than one percent. You've already made the basket, she told herself. Don't worry about the foul shot. But it was hard not to. She put her toe on the line and forced herself to breathe. The gym was silent, and she hated it. The ref gave her the ball, and she held it for a second, staring at the hoop. Just concentrate, she told herself. She took a deep breath and then she shot.

The ball hit nothing. Not the rim, not the backboard, not the net. Her cheeks burned as she backpedaled down the court.

"Yeah, Zoe!" Levi shouted. "Still a rock star!"

She tried to keep the grin off her face and failed.

She finished the game with ten points, but more importantly, Carver Harbor was victorious—in great part because the giant number thirty-three had fouled out late in the third quarter. Zoe had drawn three of those fouls. She had no idea why or how, but Coach was very pleased with her for doing it.

She hurriedly got dressed and came out of the locker room excited to see Levi. Her heart fell to the floor when she didn't see him in the gym. She looked in all directions, but he was gone. Trying not to look like she was hurrying, she hurried out into the parking lot to look for his mother's car. But it wasn't there.

"What are we, chopped liver?"

Zoe turned to see Gramma and Walter had come out the door behind her.

"Sorry. I was looking for Levi."

"I'm teasing. I can't blame you for wanting to see that nice young man." Gramma wrapped her arms around her and squeezed. "Oh, honey, I'm so proud of you."

"That was pretty amazing, champ," Walter said.

"Thanks. I'm starving. Let's go home." She led them to the car, her disappointment about Levi's absence fading.

But once she had showered, and her tummy was full, and she lay in bed looking at her phone, she couldn't stop thinking about him.

"Thanks for cheering me on tonight," she texted. Then she held her breath, feeling sick, wondering if she shouldn't have texted him. She didn't want to annoy him.

Her phone dinged. "Welcome."

Wow, what a wordsmith. "It really did help. I was nervous."

"Good."

She rolled her eyes. He was really going to make her work for this. "Did you have some important appointment you had to keep?"

He sent her a laughing emoji. "No."

She wanted to throw the phone across the room. "Are you capable of texting more than one word?"

"Yes."

She laughed out loud, and as she did, her phone dinged again with another laughing emoji.

"You're such a weirdo," she wrote, smiling in the dark.

"That's a true story."

"FOUR WORDS!" she wrote in all caps. Her heart danced in her chest. She couldn't remember the last time she'd had this much fun.

"You're welcome."

She laughed again and waited, hoping he'd say something else. Her phone was silent. After a few minutes, she typed, "I was wondering if you wanted to take me out on a real date sometime." She stared at her words, wondering if she should delete them, and then, before she lost her nerve, she pressed send.

Chapter 50

Chevon

Chevon's mom was acting suspiciously. She'd told her that she needed help with something and asked her to get dressed. Then, as Chevon was coming down the stairs, she'd looked up at her and said, "That's what you're wearing?"

Chevon stopped and stared at her. "What's wrong with this? Where are we going?"

"I'll tell you when we get there. Go make yourself presentable."

Chevon didn't move. "I am presentable."

Her mother sighed dramatically. "Go put on nice clothes and some makeup. And do something with your hair."

What was going on? Her mother walked away, and Chevon realized that she wasn't going to get an explanation, so she went back up the stairs to change.

With a little makeup on, her hair in a neat ponytail, and fresh clothes, she came back down the stairs. Her mother looked her up and down. She still didn't look impressed, but she didn't complain this time. "Come on, we're late."

What on earth was going on? She followed her mother out to the car.

As they drove away, her mom smacked her gum incessantly. Was she nervous about something? "Mom, is something wrong?"

Had her mother changed her mind? Was she whisking her away to some clinic somewhere? She knew her father still wasn't okay with everything, even though he had finally said that it was Chevon's decision.

"Everything's great." Her body language suggested otherwise, but Chevon did not argue.

She pulled onto Jason's street and started to slow down. Chevon's heart raced. The not knowing was making her ill. When they pulled into Jason's driveway, her mother said, "Don't worry, he's expecting you."

"What?"

Her mother gave her a tired look. "I didn't want your father to know where I was taking you, but Jason wanted to see you."

"Mom! You're so devious!"

"No, I'm not. And don't ever call me that again." She smiled and her voice softened. "Now, get out of my car. I love you. Go have fun with your boyfriend."

Chevon giggled at the absurdity of it all, leaned over and gave her mom a peck on the cheek, and then got out of the car. She hadn't been expecting this, but now that the opportunity had dropped into her lap, she was excited to see Jason. She walked up to his door and knocked while her mother drove away.

Jason opened the door immediately, looked her up and down, and said, "You look beautiful!"

She grinned bashfully. "Thank you," she said quietly.

He stepped outside and pulled the door shut behind him. He gave her a quick kiss, which she awkwardly accepted. It was so weird having a boyfriend. It was even weirder that said boyfriend was Jason.

"I'd invite you in, but we're already late."

She knew that he was trying to keep her away from his mother, and she didn't mind. She wasn't quite ready to deal with Mrs. DeGrave. "Late for what?"

He smiled mischievously. "You'll see. Come on."

The car hadn't even warmed up before they reached their destination. New Beginnings Church. She looked at him. "I already promised to go to church tomorrow. Do I really need to go on a Saturday too?"

He grinned and jumped out of the car. With less eagerness, she climbed out too and looked up at the church. "What, are we here to celebrate the anniversary of my great stand?"

He laughed and wrapped his arm around her waist. This sent a thrill coursing through her. "No, I hadn't even thought of that." He looked at the church. "Wow, it's been a week. That feels like a long time ago."

Sometimes it did. Sometimes it felt like just minutes ago.

He smiled down at her. "But from now on I am going to call that Chevon's Great Stand." He said the words in a deep, rumbly voice.

She giggled.

"Come on." He took her hand and led her toward the steps.

The weird man from church sat on the front steps.

"Hey, Jason. You know what's going on in there?"

"Hey, Derek. I do, but don't worry, I don't think you want to be a part of it."

What did that mean? Suddenly Chevon was scared. Were they staging some sort of religious intervention for her? She didn't know how much more Jesus she could take. But the man on the step seemed to accept this explanation, and they walked past him through the first door. As Jason opened the second door for her, before her eyes could adjust to the dimmer lighting, a bunch of people yelled, "Surprise!" and scared the tar out of her. She jumped, her hands flew to her mouth, and then she turned and punched Jason.

"Ow!" he cried.

"Sorry," she said quickly. She wiped at his chest as if trying to wipe her punch off. After years of being his buddy, it was hard to transition to being his girlfriend.

He took her hand and smiled, and she could see the affection in his eyes.

"It's not good for the baby to get so scared."

"Oh, stop it. Come on." He led her to a giant circle of chairs, almost all of which were full. Many of the women from church were there, as well as some of her friends from school. Her grandmother from out of state was there, as was her aunt. And when her eyes fell on her mother, she started crying. "Mom," she said and then stopped, at a loss for words.

Her mom started crying too. She got up and came to Chevon and wrapped her arms around her. She kissed her on the temple and then let go. "Come on, honey, sit. You have a lot of gifts to open."

Gifts! Of course. She'd figured out this was a shower, but she hadn't yet connected the dots—there would be gifts. Her eyes drifted to a table buried in pastel wrapping paper. Bunnies, elephants, ducks galore. Frogs and trains and giraffes. She giggled nervously. She had never felt so far out of her element.

Jason stepped closer and kissed her on the cheek. "This is a no-dude zone, so I'm going to leave you." He leaned even closer and whispered, "I love you. Have fun."

Zoe's grandmother got up and patted an armchair by the present table. "Go ahead, Chevon. We gave you the comfy seat."

Chevon went and sat, and when she did, an incredible peace settled over her. She didn't like crowds, she didn't love being around strangers, and she didn't like a whole bunch of people staring at her, and yet she found herself completely comfortable and content. What a bizarre experience. She wondered if it was pregnancy hormones.

"I know this is a bit early for a baby shower," Rachel said, "but we wanted to be sure you knew how much we're behind you. And now"—she swept her arm toward the table of gifts— "you'll know what you have ahead of time so you can figure out what you still need."

Chevon couldn't imagine needing anything more than what was there. But then again, she had no clue what it took to raise a baby—no matter how many very thick books her mother bought her.

"I was trying to plan some games," Rachel continued, "but then we had such an outpouring of gifts that we decided to skip the games because it might take you all day to open the presents."

Chevon sat there speechless.

Rachel clapped her hands and reached for one of the packages. "So then. Welcome to your shower. Now get to work." She handed the first package over to Chevon.

Feeling incredibly conspicuous, Chevon started unwrapping.

It was a stuffed duck. She found it rather unexciting but pretended to be delighted and held it up for all to see.

"Is that a stuffed duck?" Vicky sounded disgusted.

"It's not *just* a stuffed duck," one of the women explained. "It's a womb duck."

"A womb what?" Vicky cried.

The woman didn't answer her.

"Barbara! What on earth is a womb duck?" Vicky demanded.

The woman named Barbara looked annoyed. "A womb duck mimics the sound of the mother's heartbeat as the baby heard it in the womb. Then, when the baby is trying to fall asleep, the sound of the womb duck comforts her."

"Oh." Apparently, Vicky had deemed this a worthwhile gift.

Chapter 51

Chevon

Chevon set the womb duck aside, and Rachel started trying to push a giant box toward her. She grunted with the effort.

Zoe jumped up to help. "Why don't you let me take over the Santa duties. You go relax."

Rachel readily relinquished her position, and Zoe easily slid the giant box across the floor. Chevon reached out to help by pulling it toward her and saw what the trouble had been. This sucker was heavy. It didn't take long to find out why. A little unwrapping revealed a large wooden crib. She gasped. "Wow. Thank you." She had no idea how much a crib cost, but she thought this looked expensive. She looked the package over for a card.

"You're quite welcome," Vicky said.

The next box was a Pack 'n Play. The one after that, another Pack 'n Play.

Lauren giggled. "Don't worry, you can't have too many."

The next large box was a car seat. Again, Chevon thought about how expensive these purchases must have been. She read the card. "Dawn?"

She scanned the circle until a woman said, "That's me."

"Thank you so much."

"You're welcome."

There were more clothes than any single child could ever wear, a flood of pastel green and yellow. There were thousands of diapers, so many that Chevon started to dread that chore, but on the heels of one huge box of diapers came something called a Diaper Genie, which the women swore would save the day. There was a box of decals, which Barbara explained was a complete Noah's Ark scene. Chevon couldn't imagine her father was going to let her glue a Noah's Ark scene to one of his walls, but she said thank you just the same.

When Chevon unwrapped the breast pump, she quickly set it on the floor, sure that she would now have some bad dreams tonight.

There were baby board books and storybooks for older kids, toys, dolls, and blocks. There was a diaper bag, baby bottles, and an astonishing array of baby lotions.

When Chevon unwrapped the nipple cream, she quickly set it on the breast pump box. Yes, there were definitely going to be nightmares tonight.

She was getting exhausted, and there were still presents left. She unwrapped a giant box of wipes. Then she unwrapped another giant box of wipes. And then a third. She was now the proud owner of nearly one billion baby wipes.

Lauren tittered. "Trust me, you'll use every one of them, and then let me know, and I'll get you more."

Looking quite proud of herself, Zoe handed her a smaller package.

Chevon looked up into her eyes. "Is this from you?"

Zoe shook her head. "Oh no, I'm not this crafty. I got you one of the wipes packages."

Oh yeah, she'd known that. She'd read the card. Carefully, Chevon pulled back the wrapping paper to reveal the most perfect little knit booties. She held them up for everyone to ohh and ahh. Then she held up the matching hat and the matching sweater. Beneath those lay a knitted baby blanket, a pastel rainbow. There was no card, and her eyes scanned the circle.

Esther shyly raised her hand. "Those are from me. I didn't want to spend money on a card." Several of her cohorts giggled at this admission.

Zoe leaned over and whispered into Chevon's ear, "She started knitting those the day she found out you were pregnant."

Tears came to Chevon's eyes. So many people had believed in this baby, even before she had. What a special child this baby was going to be. Or, what a special child this baby already *was*.

When she finished unwrapping the last gift, she relaxed. She was incredibly grateful, but still she hoped the party would end soon. She was overwhelmed and exhausted. "Wow, thank you, everyone. I don't know what to say."

"Not so fast!" Rachel said, and Chevon suppressed a groan.

"We have one more round of presents." Rachel jumped up and went to the back of the sanctuary. She grabbed a wooden box that looked like an antique jewelry box. It was polished wood with ornate designs carved into it. Rachel handed it to her, and Chevon took it, not sure what she was supposed to do with it.

"Open," Rachel ordered.

Chevon flipped the lid open to see a pile of small envelopes. She picked the top one up and looked at Rachel.

Rachel sat back down. "Go ahead. Open it."

Chevon pulled a piece of paper out of the envelope and unfolded it. She read silently. "I gift you three hours of babysitting each week until your child is eighteen or I am dead, whichever comes first. Love, Rachel."

Fresh tears sprang to Chevon's eyes, and she looked up to meet Rachel's. "Am I supposed to read it out loud?" Her voice cracked.

"No need to."

"Thank you." She realized they probably didn't know if she was thanking Rachel for the letter or for not making her read it out loud. Both were true.

Rachel gave her a knowing nod.

She pulled out the second envelope. "I will watch your baby during every church service and every church event as long as I am able. And when I am no longer able, Zoe will take my place. Love, Vicky."

Chevon laughed aloud, looked at Vicky, and said, "Thank you." Vicky winked.

With trembling fingers, she opened the third envelope. "I will cook you and your family one meal each week for the first year of your baby's life. Love, Barbara."

The fourth letter read, "I will take you out for a meal once a month at a restaurant of your choice while Jason watches the baby. Love, Esther."

Tears rolled down Chevon's cheeks as she laughed again. She looked up at Esther. "Thank you."

The fifth letter: "Once you have your own home, I promise to come help you clean as often as you need it. Love, Dawn."

The sixth letter: "I will teach you how to make healthy baby food for really cheap. Love, Cathy."

And last but not least: "I commit to praying for your child every single day. Love, Vera. P.S. I have already started."

Chevon closed the box gently, embarrassed of how wet her face was. She wiped her chin on her shoulder. She had never felt such love, such gratitude. She looked up at them. "You guys are so amazing. I don't know what to say."

"You don't have to say anything," Rachel said. "This is what we're here for."

Chapter 52

Jason

J ason didn't think Pastor's sermon was terribly complicated, but he couldn't follow it. His mind kept drifting toward what was going to happen *after* church. Or what he *hoped* would happen, anyway. What he'd planned for.

He sneaked a look at Chevon. Would she be annoyed? Would she reject him? Was it too soon?

When the service finally ended, he jumped to his feet.

"Holy cow, you have to go to the bathroom or something?"

He laughed. "No, but I would like to take a little drive. Are you game?"

She shrugged. "Sure. Just not too long. I'm starving."

"We'll find some food after." He took her hand and tried not to run for the door. A few people tried to stop them for chitchat, but Jason politely made his way through them. Finally they were outside, and he opened his car door for her.

She looked up at him. "Are you okay?"

"Of course. Hop in."

He drove her to Fort Wagner.

"What are we doing here?"

"I don't know. I was looking for a beautiful spot."

"Well, this is a beautiful spot in the *summer*. I'm not sure it's that great right now."

When he got out of the car, he understood what she meant. The wind whipped across the open landscape, stabbing his face with a million tiny ice picks. He considered changing his plan but then decided to forge ahead. He didn't know where else he could go, and he didn't want to lose his nerve. He opened her door and offered her his hand. "This won't take long."

Her eyes were huge. "Jason, what on earth are we doing?"

Doubts swarmed in his brain, and he tried to focus on his heart instead. "I wanted someplace beautiful, someplace we would remember."

She gasped. "Oh my goodness!"

"Don't worry, I'm not going to propose to you."

Her face relaxed. She giggled. "Don't scare me like that." This hurt his feelings, and apparently it showed on his face because she hurried to add, "It's not that I don't want to marry you. But I'm sixteen. I think my father would have to agree to it, and you know the chances of that."

He had planned to get down on one knee, but now that they stood in the snow, he changed his mind. He reached into his pocket and pulled out the small velvet box.

"For someone who's not proposing, you're sure acting like someone who's proposing."

He snapped the box open. "This is a tiny diamond."

Her hands flew to her mouth.

"But it's a real diamond. I can't afford a good one right now—"

She made a weird squealing sound. Sort of like a cat.

He would've laughed if he wasn't so focused.

"How did you afford any diamond at all?"

He tried not to let his annoyance show. "You sure know how to muck up a romantic gesture."

Her eyes were still asking the question.

"My dad helped. Now, will you let me do this?"

Her eyes twinkling, she nodded.

"This is a ring to fill the gap between now and the next ring—the real ring. I wanted to come to someplace beautiful to promise you that I will propose to you ..." The wind blew in his face, and he turned away from it, gasping for air.

He turned back to Chevon. "I will ask to be your husband as soon as I can. I know we're too young. But I wanted you to know that I'm in this forever. I love you, Chevon. I didn't know that was coming, but it happened, and I'm not even sorry that any of this happened." He turned and gasped for more air. "You don't have to say anything right now, but I wanted you to know that I am serious about this. I am committing to you for the rest of my life. And there is a real proposal and a real ring coming." He stopped and waited for her to say something. He felt as if his whole future hung on her next word.

She pulled her hands away from her face to reveal a giant smile. She wrapped her arms around his neck and pulled him toward her. Her whole body was shivering. She pressed her lips to his, and they felt so warm in the icy wind. She pulled away, her eyes sparkling. "I very much look forward to that proposal, Jason DeGrave."

Books by Robin Merrill

New Beginnings
Knocking
Kicking
Searching
Knitting
Working
Splitting

Greater Life
Forgive and Remember
A Good Day to Live

Shelter Trilogy
Shelter
Daniel
Revival

Piercehaven Trilogy
Piercehaven
Windmills
Trespass

Standalone Stories
Commack
Grace Space: A Direct Sales Tale (the original Gertrude story)

Gertrude, Gumshoe Cozy Mystery Series
Introducing Gertrude, Gumshoe
Gertrude, Gumshoe: Murder at the Thrift Store
Gertrude, Gumshoe and the VardSale Villain
Gertrude, Gumshoe: Slam Is Murder
Gertrude, Gumshoe: Gunslinger City
Gertrude, Gumshoe and the Clearwater Curse

Gertrude in South Dakota
Gertrude, Gumshoe: S'more Murder
Gertrude, Gumshoe: Haunted Hotel
Gertrude, Gumshoe: Cowboy Shoot

Wing and a Prayer Mysteries
The Whistle Blower
The Showstopper
The Pinch Runner
The Prima Donna Featuring Gertrude, Gumshoe